# Vista Chinesa

**TATIANA SALEM LEVY** is a writer, essayist, and researcher at Universidade Nova de Lisboa. Her first novel, *The House in Smyrna* (also published by Scribe and translated by Alison Entrekin), won Brazil's most generous literary award — the São Paulo Prize for Literature — for a debut work. She lives in Lisbon, and is a columnist for the newspaper *Valor Econômico*.

**ALISON ENTREKIN** has translated over forty books from the Portuguese, including the classics *City of God* by Paulo Lins, *Near to the Wild Heart* by Clarice Lispector, and *My Sweet Orange Tree* by José Mauro de Vasconcelos. In 2019 she was awarded the New South Wales Premier's Translation Prize and PEN medallion for the body of her work.

# VISTA CHINESA

## Tatiana Salem Levy

Translated by Alison Entrekin

SCRIBE

*Melbourne • London*

Scribe Publications
2 John St, Clerkenwell, London, WC1N 2ES, United Kingdom
18–20 Edward St, Brunswick, Victoria 3056, Australia

First published in Portuguese as *Vista Chinesa*
by Todavia in 2021

Published by Scribe in Australia and New Zealand 2022
Published by Scribe in the UK and North America 2023

Typeset in Adobe Caslon by the publishers

Printed and bound in the UK by CPI Group (UK) Ltd,
Croydon CR0 4YY

Scribe is committed to the sustainable use of natural resources
and the use of paper products made responsibly from those
resources

978 1 914484 22 3 (UK edition)
978 1 922585 28 8 (Australian edition)
978 1 922586 73 5 (ebook)

Catalogue records for this book are available from the National
Library of Australia and the British Library.

This project has been assisted by the Australian Government
through the Australia Council for the Arts, its arts funding and
advisory body.

scribepublications.co.uk
scribepublications.com.au

*To Vicente and Esther*

'I write this very decidedly out of despair over my body and over a future with this body.'

Franz Kafka, *Diaries*

Antonia and Martim, my loves,

While you watch a cartoon, I wonder how to begin this letter. I write, erase, rewrite, get distracted looking at you. So many good things come to mind that I hesitate to go dredging up the past. If your father knew I'd decided to tell you what happened to me, he'd say, Forget it. At first, I believed it was possible. More than him, more than anyone, I saw forgetting as the only way to move on. I spent hours devising strategies to expunge the reality of what happened, as if I could go back to being the same Júlia as before. But there are things that, even after they've happened, keep on happening. They don't let you forget, because they repeat themselves daily. That's why I can't shake the idea that you know. You inhabited my womb, fed at my breast; you bathe with me, sleep in my arms, we snuggle up on the sofa together, so you know, just as I know every time I look at myself in the mirror. You just don't know the words.

Last night I tossed and turned in bed, thinking: What if I die without telling them? At first I thought it would be for the best. Then I convinced myself that if I didn't, the day would come when you would hear a rumour, you'd discover a tip of the story, then perhaps another and another — but there would always be a piece missing. The truth would be missing, because like this, the way I'm going to tell it now, I've never told anyone.

I can imagine your shock if you ever end up reading this letter. It won't be easy to see your own mother shattered. First and foremost, I want you to understand something that took me a while to accept myself: if at any point it appears that I've gone insane, know that no one is truthful in sanity. No one. Not even your mother.

It was a Tuesday. The year, 2014. Brazil, the country of the future, seemed very close to fulfilling its destiny. In less than a month it would host the World Cup and, two years later, Rio de Janeiro would become the Olympic capital. Nothing pointed to disaster, neither in the city, which was on the cover of every newspaper and magazine, nor in my life. There was no way anything could go wrong, not least because our destinies were entwined. My office — at the time, just Cadu and myself — had won the public tender to design the golf course clubhouse. After one hundred and twelve years, golf was returning to the Olympics.

I remember what day it was because I'd left a note on my desk: *Tuesday, meeting with City Hall.* More precisely, our first meeting with the Secretary for the Environment, the owner of the land in Barra da Tijuca, and the international golf course designer, all together.

Severino, the doorman of my building, still wasn't back from lunch and, as usual, I hid the key in a pot plant by the stairs. I never take anything with me when I go for a run, just my mobile in the waistband of my leggings and headphones in my ears. Up to that point, I remember everything, from the door of the building banging shut, me looking to see if any cars were coming, crossing the street, turning right, then left, passing in front of the Horto bakery and the newsstand. But from the moment I started up the hill to the Vista Chinesa lookout, the details are less precise.

I can't say if there were other people, if there were more birds than usual, if monkeys crossed my path, or if the sun, which was shining brightly, disappeared behind a cloud at some point. When I run I switch off from the world. Nothing catches my attention — not the forest on either side of the road, or passers-by, or even the breathtaking view from the top. I only come back to reality when the metallic voice on my phone interrupts the music to announce my average speed and the number of kilometres I've run.

While my mind travels far, my body, on the contrary, is always present. My leg muscles contract, the pain arrives, searing, and I almost want to give up. But it has never happened. No matter how gruelling it is, I am incapable of telling myself Today I'm tired; today my body can't take it. I force it to endure.

But with the pain comes pleasure, too, the endorphins spread, my blood circulates faster, and I feel I'm achieving my goal.

I repeated this ritual twice a week. The only difference here was the hour: I never ran in the afternoons. In the mornings there were more people, and I hated hearing my parents or Michel telling me that I shouldn't run to Vista Chinesa, as it was deserted. Rio de Janeiro, even now, even being the most talked-about city in the world, has never stopped being dangerous. But until that Tuesday the danger was an abstraction to me.

Without me intuiting or foreseeing anything, without me thinking It's deserted, or seeing someone strange in the distance, without feeling a scrap of fear, a shiver, a bad feeling, without me receiving any kind of sign from the outside world, danger suddenly appeared behind me. He was short, strong, put a pistol to my head, and said, Follow me, his voice blending with Daniela Mercury's, his hand squeezing my arm, interrupting my run and dragging me into the forest, that beautiful, exuberant jungle, sung of in the most beautiful poems, exalted in tourist guidebooks and in the choice of Rio de Janeiro as the host city for the 2016 Olympic Games, that forest that everyone says is what makes the difference; after all, lots of capital cities have beaches, but a forest like that, tropical, verdant, immense, only in Rio, that leafy jungle, home to toucans, snakes, and monkeys, that forest that exhales a sickly sweet smell of jack fruit, that forest that everyone admires on their way up to Vista Chinesa and which I almost never notice, because when I run I switch off from the world, that forest became my hell.

The very instant my feet left the asphalt and began to tread on the fallen leaves in the humidity of the forest, I noticed that something about his hand on my arm felt unpleasant. Without turning my head, I glanced sideways and saw that he was wearing gloves. In the following seconds, or minutes, I can't be sure anymore, all I could do was look at the gloves. The branches scratching my body, his voice, the sun disappearing between the trees, his threats, the sound of our footsteps in the forest, everything becoming diluted and losing its original form; all I could see was the gloves. I need to make an effort, I thought, I need to remember everything, just the gloves isn't enough, but even now the only thing I can see clearly is the gloves. The rest was just blurry images. Later I saw other things. I saw pieces, fragments of that moment: a clearing a belt a whack my throat leaves in the sky a mouth moving a tongue shoes a bare chest a whack a little bird a punch a belt leaves falling from the sky another punch gag reflex bad taste a cloud pain it's going to break midges a bad smell inside another whack aside from pain pain pain one jackfruit two jackfruits lots of jackfruits a face the details of a face a face distorting a face.

It's hard to describe a face. It's true even for a familiar face that you haven't seen for a while. My grandma's, for example, I can only reassemble with a photograph.

Sometimes I wonder, doubtful: what did Grandma look like? The image of a diffuse face appears and takes on contours, but when I try to focus on a particular part — her eyes, her nose — I can't, it's as if the parts only exist together, as a whole.

What matters most about a person: the whole or the details? What we remember or what we forget?

Over the next few days, I had to describe the man's face. The colour of his skin, the shape of his mouth, the size of his nose, the colour of his eyes, the texture of his hair, any and every distinctive feature, a scar, a mole, a mark, a tattoo. That was when everything began to grow confused, details came and went, mingled, swam into and out of focus. I had to remember, and the memory escaped me, like an image that comes to you in the middle of the night and quickly darkens if you try to hold onto it, or like a proof that has been left too long in a developing tank.

It's maddening when words don't stick to the image. All cracks are exasperating, but this one hurts my body. I want to shout, Please, give me the right word, then someone says, There isn't one, there's no such thing as the right word, but I don't believe it, I think there's a right word for everything, and if you talk talk talk you eventually find it.

The right words might be: *I was raped.* Your mother was raped. Me, your mother, I was raped. It happened. I was. Raped. Raped. R-a-p-e-d.

It's what you're going to hear from someone in a

casual conversation, one glass too many, a more intimate conversation, or even from me: Mummy was raped, did you know? But something's still missing. I still need to explain what the word meant to me at that moment and in all of the following moments over the last five years in which I became your mother. It was already night when my feet returned to the asphalt, now bare, gashed by branches. Finally I'd found the road; I don't know how long I spent lost in the forest, disoriented, wandering this way and that, watching the sky grow dark at a frightening speed, until I did, I found the asphalt, and the asphalt had never seemed so soft, so welcoming, so close. I was alive, that's what I thought: I'm alive. It was the only thing that mattered, I wanted to get to a safe place and tell people: I'm alive.

I imagined that my parents, my brother, and Michel were looking for me. I'd told Cadu that I was going for a run to Vista Chinesa before going to the meeting; for sure I wasn't going to be late, imagine, no way was I going to be late for our first meeting with City Hall about the Olympic golf course club house. And, when I say I won't be late, I'm never late. For sure he'd called my mother or Michel, everyone was worried, retracing the route from my place to Vista Chinesa dozens of time. I'd most likely see them along the way.

I caught a glimpse of someone heading downhill on a bike, so fast that they probably barely noticed I was there. A short time later, I looked up and saw a forest ranger. I assumed he'd ask if I needed anything, but he kept walking as if I didn't exist, and I confess that, despite my dismay, I felt relieved. I didn't want to speak to anyone, I just wanted to get home and tell everyone I was alive. When I was almost in Horto, a couple approached me; I quickly dismissed them with my hand, a curt gesture, making it clear that I didn't want contact, and it was only then that I realised my shirt was torn. As I touched it, I saw the marks on my stomach that ran all the way up to my arms. I put a hand on my face, and it hurt. My nose and my eye were swollen.

I started to cry. That healthy body that had run to Vista Chinesa in leggings and a T-shirt, that could run six kilometres in forty minutes, had become a hurt, fragile body, covered in marks. That was when I stopped thinking that I was alive and began to wonder what living would be like from then on, how I was going to work, eat, bathe; I'd clearly never be able to sleep again, or kiss Michel, or have sex with Michel, and what about the children I wanted so badly, what was I going to do? I was alive, but still didn't know if life would be possible.

My dad and brother were heading up the hill by car as I turned left at the top of my street. We just missed each other. I continued on downhill for almost ten minutes by myself, going very slowly, my feet bare and scratched. Still at a distance, I saw a woman at the door to my building. I couldn't immediately tell who it was. It was only when I drew closer that I recognised the dress, a dress she wore often.

Diana came running towards me and I felt that I could switch off, surrender my body to someone else, to that friend who was so dear, who hugged me tightly, tenderly, who welcomed me with her slender body, and for a few seconds I passed out, which was the best thing that could have happened to me just then, to be unconscious in her warm, caring arms.

As I slowly came to, I heard her shouting to Severino, who helped carry me up the stairs to the first floor. They placed me on the sofa, the door closed, Severino had gone, and I lay there, waiting. Diana picked up the phone and told my mother, Júlia's here.

I saw that she looked drawn, her back curved, her gaze lost. We hugged one another and cried, as if I could pass a little of my dilacerated body to her and she could give me a little of her intact body. She asked me if I wanted to talk, and I replied with a gesture. Shower, do you want one? Again, I couldn't articulate a thing. So she said, Let's go, and took me to the bathroom. She turned on the tap and said, It's OK, I'll help you. What I most wanted was to take my clothes off, but what I most wanted to avoid was being naked. The part of me that had died was my body, and my body was what was most alive, screaming with a gaping mouth, teeth on show.

I lifted up my arms and she took off my T-shirt. My bra had stayed behind in the forest. Tears kept streaming from her eyes and she suddenly apologised; of course she wanted to come across as strong, she didn't want to show me that she was frightened, horrified, she wanted to seem as natural as possible, be reassuring, tell me that everything would soon be alright, but none of it was natural, and she crumbled. We hugged again. The water will calm you, she said, but she must have wanted to say: The water will wash that filth off you.

I didn't have the strength to take off my leggings, so Diana did it for me. My thighs had as many marks as my stomach did; I didn't know if I could handle that body that had never been so mine and so little mine at the same time. I want to take it back, exchange it: this body's different now. When she went to pull off my underwear, I grabbed her hands. I was ashamed. Terribly ashamed, as if every detail, including the worst, of what had just happened to me was written between my legs. As if, no. It was. Anyone could tell just by looking at my naked body.

The warm water was carrying me far away, dissolving the solidity of my shoulders, my legs. I stood there motionless with my eyes closed for a long while, until the tears returned, uncontrollable. With one hand on the wall and the other on the shower door, I slid down until I was sitting. A short time later, Diana got in the shower with me. Her hands on my head, lathering up the shampoo, was my first joy. The second was the water running over my face with the bubbles.

I perked up a little, and before I knew it I was trying to scrub off my skin, that impure layer, with the sponge, all I wanted was new skin. You learn early on that skin regenerates, it flakes off and grows back — just think about when you sunbathe or exfoliate. Therefore, I could, all I had to do was scrub hard and the evil would leave and I'd be me again, intact.

Just as I turned off the shower, I heard the doorbell. Wrapped in a towel, Diana ran to answer it, distraught. I opened the shower door and threw myself into my mother's arms, into the embrace I'd been longing for from the second I'd felt the cool metal of the pistol against my head.

It was the first time I'd spoken. I didn't need to say anything, the rape was there for all to see on my face, in the marks, but she hadn't seen me arrive, she hadn't seen the torn clothes, and I wanted to make sure she knew, so I said one thing and fell silent. I remember wondering if it was worse to be in my place or in hers; a pain that couldn't be touched, the impossibility of physical, palpable suffering, the void that separated us. I would watch my mother lose weight over the coming days, but she would never know in her body the torment that I had experienced, and there couldn't be anything worse than the tangible lack of knowledge of your child's pain.

Diana came back into the bathroom with a pale face, harried, saying she was sorry, she'd just called Dr Brito, our gynaecologist, and he'd said that I shouldn't shower under any circumstances; first, I had to go get a rape kit exam done. I don't know how I didn't think of it earlier, she said, and repeated over and over, Shit, shit. I glanced at the shower and saw my wet underwear on the floor. My mother followed my gaze and understood. Too late.

I wanted to reassure them both, shift the blame from Diana. Even if I hadn't showered, I wasn't doing the exam, I said, God forbid that I should have to set foot in a police station, that story ended there, my story, ours, no one else's. It was my privacy, my torment, and the sooner I put a full stop to it, the better. To be honest, I continued, there's no way I could do the exam, I can't imagine myself lying on a bed, someone touching me.

But Dr Brito asked you to be at the São Vicente Clinic in two hours, she said, he needs to examine you. So it isn't over, I thought, it is just the beginning. I left the bathroom wrapped in a towel, and went to get dressed in my room.

When Dad and José arrived, furious, they already knew. My father, in the manner of his Syrian family, had his hands in the air, crying openly, at the top of his voice, My little girl, my little girl, his broad arms wrapping around me, suffocating me against his chest. My brother just hollered, I'm going to get that son of a bitch, I'm going to smash that son of a bitch, he's going to pay for what he did, that son of a bitch. But the minute Dad let me go, José hugged me, too; tenderness overcame anger. Everyone was thinking the same thing I had been when I came out of the forest: I could have been dead, but I was alive.

I told José that I'd showered and that it would be

impossible to find the man, but he was obsessed with the idea of catching him. He went through my things in the bathroom, carefully putting everything in a plastic bag, saying, There has to be some proof of him here — a fingerprint, a strand of hair, something. He was wearing gloves, I said.

Dad reassured him, We'll see about that later, we'll see what can be done later, for now we're going to stay here with Júlia. I remember looking at the four of them and thinking that if I hadn't gone for a run to Vista Chinesa that afternoon, they wouldn't be there, suffering with me, or worse, because of me. To this day, I think that if I hadn't gone out, my life wouldn't have been shattered, but I'd hate it if someone said that to me, if someone had asked in a reprimanding tone, C'mon, what were you doing up there on a Tuesday afternoon, have you no sense of danger, don't you know what Rio de Janeiro's like, do you think you live in Tokyo or Stockholm, their inquisitorial gaze telling me that it was basically my fault, because if I hadn't gone for a run alone, none of it would have happened and no one would be suffering because of me; I'd have spared myself and everyone else. My head was lost in these suppositions when Michel arrived.

I was afraid of how he'd react, afraid he'd blame me, be disgusted, repulsed, or angry. It was a relief to see that, at least at first, there were tears in his eyes and love in his gestures. I had the impression that, instead of pushing us apart, pain might unite us.

Our two years together had placed us at an impasse. He wanted to shack up together, those were his words, but he thought it was too early to have children. We've got time, he'd say, let's wait for the right time, while I was pressed for time. I was turning thirty-five and wanted to get pregnant soon, but suddenly time became everything but pressed. It was suspended, and would remain so until I didn't know when. Trauma, a word I'd hear from the police dozens of times, interrupts everything around it; it interrupts the world itself, shuffles time, memory, and you're swept out of the landscape.

Cadu got there just as we were leaving, already in the foyer. I bowed my head, ashamed, as if my darkest intimacy had been made public. A fight going on, the whole time, between the body that was no longer mine and the body that had never been so mine. I wished Cadu wasn't there, and the feeling reiterated the fact that I wasn't going to report the incident, that I didn't want to talk to anyone else about what had happened. I needed to push forward, get up, cling to a buoy in the churning sea, to the words that made sense of it all: I'm alive, and that's what matters.

When I was about to get into the car I turned back, wanting to know how the meeting had gone. At first, Cadu was silent, then he replied, It went really well, Júlia, they loved the project. After a short pause, he continued, But don't think about that now, take a few days off, relax, I'll skipper the boat until you think you're ready. No, I said, I want to think about it, it's precisely what I want to think about, nothing else. He agreed with a nod, saw the desperation in my eyes — anything to get me out of the hole I was in, and work, in my case, was the best thing. After my body, it was my next biggest obsession.

Bleeding, I told the receptionist at the São Vicente Clinic Emergency Department. I was led to a small room. Diana came in with me. Everyone else waited outside. Dr Brito arrived a few minutes later and gave me a hug. I know it's unpleasant, he said, but I need to examine you. I lay down on the bed, spread my legs, and felt Diana's hand squeezing mine. A bit wider, he told me. I complied. The cold room, the cold bed; I felt my cold body on the moist forest floor, in another space, another time, but also in the same space, at the same time, the cold forest on the hospital bed, the cold forest in so many other places, a time spent in so many other times.

Dr Brito inserted the speculum, and shortly said there were no tears in the uterus, which was very positive. I was and I wasn't there, inhabiting a fluid state between the presence and absence of my own body. I became distressed when he mentioned the difficulty of getting the antiretroviral cocktail at a private hospital. The problem wasn't the cocktail in itself, but the possibility, which was dawning on me for the first time, that I might have been contaminated with a disease — AIDS or any other. Then

I came to my senses and asked a bunch of questions, which he answered with great patience and kindness, always reassuring me, saying that everything was going to be OK. Even though I knew it wasn't true, I needed to believe that it was, I needed to hear that it was.

After the examination, I was taken to another room, where people were beginning to arrive one after another. Before I knew it, there were suddenly seven, eight, maybe ten or eleven of us in the hospital room, friends were talking in loud voices, and all I could think about was getting out of there when Dr Brito asked me if I wanted to sleep at the clinic. My look of desperation must have answered for me, because he quickly added that if I preferred to go home, he'd give me a prescription for tranquilisers.

Diana, a kind of shadow of mine in the days that followed, phoned a friend who worked in the public healthcare system and requested the cocktail. Two hours later, there it was, those enormous, nauseating pills that I'd have to shove down my throat for two weeks.

I remember thinking that if I didn't take the cocktail, I could erase it all. What if I pretended nothing had happened? What if I convinced myself nothing had happened? Then nothing would have happened. I'd stop taking the cocktail, because nothing had happened, it was just a nightmare, a mistake, a poorly placed comma that I could now dislodge from my story. But then I'd look at the pill and swallow it, petrified.

The people didn't stop talking. Their voices blended together — some high, some low, mingling and rolling into a ball in my head. It was the first time I'd heard those voices, autonomous, bodiless, that assumed a presence even when there was no one around. Later, I would hear them quite often.

A nurse arrived, stuck a needle in my right arm, and took several tubes of blood. The sickly aroma of jack fruit came to me mixed with *his* smell, the man's, with another smell that I couldn't identify but knew was from the forest, a smell that I picked up not just in my nostrils but also in my stomach, in my saliva, a smell that impregnated several parts of my body and came back to me over and over, the physical memory of that Tuesday: revulsion, a different kind of distress to the kind that constricts your chest. The nurse was still there with the needle in my vein when I turned to one side and vomited.

The voices had disappeared. I heard the silence, theirs and mine. The certainty that no matter how much I talked I'd never manage to express the turmoil inside me also brought me the certainty of solitude. The certainty that we're alone — not just me, but all of us.

What kind of gloves, they would ask me later, what colour gloves, are you sure, do you remember properly, what kind of gloves, what colour gloves, thick or thin, black or blue, are you sure you're not mistaken, are you sure the gloves were like that, what kind of gloves, what colour gloves, now you're not sure anymore, now I'm not sure anymore, what colour gloves, what kind of gloves, a person who's been through trauma can either remember everything, the details, including what kind of gloves, what colour gloves, or they forget almost everything, how much am I making up, how can I be sure they were like that, the kind of gloves, the colour of the gloves, make an effort, if I remember the colour blue five times and the colour black two times, does that mean the gloves were blue, or do we repeat the fantasy more than our actual memory, what kind of gloves, what colour gloves, his fingers were protected, thick or thin, were they torn, were they long or short, what kind of gloves, what colour gloves?

It was Dr Brito who handed me a piece of paper with the name and contact details of the person we should see if we wanted to report it.

The next day, when I woke up, still under the effect of the tranquilisers, my parents and José were already at my place. Michel had slept over. I couldn't remember my dreams, which was rare, probably as a result of the medication. I'm alive, I thought, relieved. Whenever the memory returned, and it was all the time, I repeated the mantra: I'm alive. In the forest, the feeling that I was close to death was strong. There were moments when I told myself, I hope he's satisfied, I hope it's good for him, I hope he gets his rocks off, he doesn't get upset, he isn't disappointed, but he lets me live. I thought, Let him do what he wants — it's the only way he'll leave.

The voices, their voices, grew louder in my head. I needed people to be there as much as I needed them not to be there. Have a seat, said my father, before telling me they'd talked and come to the conclusion that I should go to the police. The perpetrator had to be caught. I stood immediately. I didn't even want to hear of it. Please, let me wake up, I'm not going to think about it now, in fact, I don't want to think about it. I already have, the matter's dead. Let it go. Forget it. I just want to forget it, I said. I'm going to forget it.

I went back to my room and fell asleep again. Two hours later, they were still there, on the same topic, and I was trying hard to be patient. Until José said, You should do it for others, too — for other women, he corrected himself. You need to report it, the guy can't be left at large out there. Who's to say you were the only one, or will be the only one? For the first time, an argument touched me. I looked at the four of them, and saw how much they were suffering. The dark circles under their eyes, their weary faces. No matter how alone I was, I wasn't the only one.

It became apparent that we all needed to cling to an objective in order to get back to the surface. To breathe. Theirs was to contact the police, report it, catch the guy. I agreed to go ahead with it, certain I'd be doing it for them, and doing something for them was, at that point, what I could do for myself.

Dad pulled the crumpled paper out of his pocket and called the police. That same afternoon, the officers would be there. José and Michel would be at work. My parents, Diana, and I would be present.

I heard their voices when they came in, the same ones that anyone would have heard, but in my head they grew louder, mingled, became independent of their bodies. At times I made out the voice of a woman asking how I was and if they could come in, saying, We don't want to disturb you, but the male voices blended together and I couldn't tell who was saying what.

In a row, I first saw an older man, who sat at the desk. Then a woman with waist-length, straightened hair took a seat on the edge of the bed, almost on my feet. Then two men, one very muscular. This was the team that was going to oversee my case.

I asked my parents to leave — I couldn't be objective with them around — while Diana stood smoking a cigarette at the window. The woman explained that she would ask me several questions. I know it's a painful process, she said, but I need as many details as possible to find the assailant. One of the men standing introduced himself as the records clerk and asked if he could take a seat. It was the woman who led the conversation, and she told me that the man at the desk would do an identikit sketch.

I refer to them as men and woman, because although I knew their names at the time, I can't remember them now. The precision they asked of me in those hours, of which I thought I was capable, was lost with each day that passed.

When the clerk sat down, I noticed that he had a gun. When the woman got up to go to the bathroom, I saw that she did, too. I presumed that the muscular man leaning against the wall also had one. I tried hard not to panic, repeating, behind what I was saying out loud: They're here to protect me, they're the police, they're not criminals.

Diana lit another cigarette.

The woman asked me for a full account: Tell me everything that comes to mind, how it started, where you were, what time it was, what he looked like, how he approached you, what he was wearing, his physical features, what he did to you, if he was armed, what his voice was like, and at the end I'll ask you questions.

It was the first time I'd told the story in so much detail, at first, in such a technical and objective manner that I felt like I wasn't saying anything. But as I talked, time became tangled, as if I didn't know the order of events. When had he made me suck his dick, before or after he punched me or my attempt to get away? I stuttered, hesitated, and then she told me that a statement should be made right after the crime. The more time goes by, the more jumbled one's memory becomes.

When she saw how hard it was for me and the uncertainty that was beginning to set in, she decided to move on to the sketch. Little by little, I understood that it was like putting together a puzzle. First, you need to draw the shape of the face, long and oval in this case, then the strongest features — scars, a beard, or accessories — and, last of all, fill in the eyes, nose, mouth, eyebrows, hair.

The sketch artist held up the page and asked if that's what the mouth was like. When I said it wasn't, he asked more questions and went back to drawing.

Wider?

Narrower.

Were there any blemishes?

No.

Was the top well-defined?

What do you mean?

Did it have a sharp outline?

A little. I mean, no. I mean, yes.

No or yes?

Maybe. Yes. But not much.

Black?

White.

Mixed race?

White.

Olive complexion?

Maybe.

Maybe?

Yes. White, olive complexion.

Eyes?

Can we continue another day? I'm tired, I told the woman practically sitting on my feet.

I've never understood if madness comes all at once or little by little, if a mad person is born mad, if they go mad from one day to the next, or if it happens slowly, and when is it that you realise you're going mad, or that you're almost there, or do you never realise it, and if you ask, is it because you're not mad yet? I wonder every day if I've gone or if I'm going mad. It happened a few years ago, then there were the Olympics, and they went well, inexplicably well, but only for a month, because the Olympics in Rio were Rio suspended from itself, or the glimmer of a utopia, the makeup you know how to put on so well but only once in a while, and then the city went downhill, the country went downhill, politics emptied of projects under the sole pretext of catching corrupt politicians and businessmen, corrupt politicians and businessmen were arrested in Rio at the same time that the city was becoming acquainted with its own hell, for the first time not even Rio was capable of saving Rio, which slowly went mad, while I too may have gone mad, or am going mad, but no one sees my madness, then Michel and I got married, we had you, we're ridiculously happy, now when people look at me they no longer see the body of a woman destroyed, they see the body of a woman who's had two children and didn't stop running even when she was pregnant, they see the body of a woman who had a normal birth and a C-section, Antonia was about to be born when her heart sped up, Martim was already out, and suddenly an anaesthetic, an incision, my hands bound as if on a cross and the baby girl wailing, the body that breastfed, one baby on each breast, people look at me and think, Wow, what an intact body, they don't even remember what happened or, when they do, they weigh it up and say, But she got it all afterwards, she got married, gave birth, she's a great mother, she lives in a lovely home and she's beautiful, look at that body, you'd never know it had been dilacerated, torn apart, fragmented, you'd never know that this woman was once a nervous wreck, no one sees what I'm thinking, no one knows I'm going mad or possibly already have, or maybe they know and I don't know that they know, no, they don't know, no one knows, I'm not even sure myself, it's so hard to know, I've put myself back together, I haven't put myself back together, I've almost put myself back together, I'll never put myself back together, I'm still in pieces, I've gone mad, I'm going mad, when they were in my belly did my children sense an intact body or a splintered body?, you're both beautiful, perfect children, but will you be intact on the inside or, because you received nourishment and energy from a splintered body, will you also have a splintered soul?, is what I see of you what you are?, is what others see of me what I am?, because you lived in my belly for nine months do you know that a man once entered me by force, with so much force that he touched me right there, on the uterus where you grew?, do parents pass on their traumas to their children even if we don't say anything?, at the week-twelve ultrasound the doctor said, One's a boy, the other one's hidden, and I immediately remembered the Mexican clairvoyant, *son dos niños iguales*, they're two identical children, and breathed a sigh of relief, but then in the week-twenty ultrasound the doctor said, How lovely, a girl and a boy, you can celebrate, and Michel did, he really wanted a girl, more than anything a girl, and I pretended to be happy, but over the following days the nausea came back, heartburn, churning stomach, tiredness, and it wasn't because of the pregnancy, it was the news, news of the girl moving around inside me and me thinking, Not a girl, and then me telling myself that I shouldn't think these things because babies feel everything, it says so in the literature, if the mother suffers they suffer, if the mother smiles they smile, all the mother, always the mother, are you sure, doctor, are you sure you aren't mistaken?, isn't his willy just tucked away, doctor, can you have another look?, the doctor smiled and I looked deep into his eyes, opening my eyes wide, and said, Doctor, when they grow up, this boy and this girl, I'm going to have to tell them that their mother was raped, then the doctor stopped smiling and Michel looked uncomfortable, where had I got that from in a moment of joy?, we were there to celebrate, not dredge up the past, why bring it up if we'd already overcome the trauma, if we'd forgotten the pain?, now it was all happiness, a boy and a girl were on their way, twins is all a couple wants, and in the silence I repeated, Doctor, when they grow up, this boy and this girl, I'm going to have to tell them, your mother was raped, and the doctor suddenly looked at me and sighed, ah, This idea that our children have to know everything, you could just not tell them, to be honest, if I were you I wouldn't, then he wiped my belly plastered with gel clean and told us we could go, we just had to wait for the report at reception, congratulations again, twins, a boy and a girl, and he shook Michel's hand hard, and I didn't know, I don't know if I'm going mad or if I'm already mad, it must be hard to tell.

It was the first time Márcia had come to my apartment. She tried to hug me, but I hesitated, I wouldn't have been able to bear that hug, I'd already collapsed so many times, now I wanted to pull myself together, so I gave her a kiss on each cheek as we do at the practice. I thought it would be better if she sat in the armchair, which I had positioned with its back to the chaise longue, where I lay down.

In my first three years of therapy, I barely said a word, sometimes I'd arrive mute and leave mute, sometimes I'd blurt out, I'm leaving, in the middle of the session, sometimes I wanted to give up, paying to be silent makes no sense, that silence, one of us with her back to the other, what should I say, why should I speak, speak as if I were alone but with a shadow behind me, a shadow that from time to time would highlight what I'd said, zero in on a sentence, a word; she was interested in what was out of place and would spiral around it, another path starting from the rock in the middle of the path, and it was only after three years that I began to talk, and then I didn't stop, I'd arrive talking, I'd leave talking, I wanted extra sessions, the ones I had didn't feel like enough, I wanted to talk to her around the clock, and suddenly she had called me, it was her idea to come to my place to hear me, and there she was, sitting in my armchair, and I couldn't talk, I didn't want to talk.

The silence was like going back to the start, an erasure of the years of analysis. It took all of my previous issues, my exaggerated relationship with my father, my dilemmas with Michel, my concerns about work, my existential crises, my questions, my doubts, my obsessions, and tossed them all in the bin. The silence told me that those seven years that I had previously thought so worthwhile didn't matter at all anymore.

Of all that we had thought about together, concluded together, what could help me understand what had happened?

My first words were, It's over, and then I reassumed my silence. A few minutes later, I repeated, It's over. So many things were over — my body, my work, my relationship, the things I wasn't sure about, my issues, my life was over. It's over. It was the only thing I could say, always with a long pause between repetitions, the pause required to hold back my tears. And each time she tried to ask me a question, each time she tried to get me to say more, I would interrupt her and say:

It's over.

It's *over*.

It's *OVER*.

After an hour in which I just repeated the same words or remained silent, I noticed that her body was moving in the armchair, she was going to get up. I could always tell the moment she was going to get up, when she would say the same thing with which she ended every session. Then she moved, stood, picked up her bag, and said, We'll continue. At that instant I felt tremendous anger. I hated her, hated her for having come to me, hated her for wanting to hear me, hated her for existing, hated her for leaving, hated her for not having understood anything, I hated that everything was over, I hated that everything went on.

That was my despair. The world went on, and my body, too, my work, my relationship, the things I wasn't sure about, my issues. My life was still there, even though it was over. She left, and it was only after the door closed that I began to think about the words that had accompanied me on my way home from the forest: I'm alive.

———

No, his nose wasn't like that, it wasn't so wide, it was narrower, the holes in his nose were narrower, that's right, nostrils, no, not like that, why don't you do what I'm saying?, am I sure?, of course I'm sure, that nose was poking me, I remember the nose, that is, I think I remember, now you're confusing me, you keep telling me that I mustn't remember, that I've been through a traumatic situation and that in traumatic situations people forget, so now I'm not sure, but his nose wasn't that wide, I'm sure, I've told you about a hundred times he wasn't black, some things you don't forget, he was white, maybe a little olive-skinned, but not black, and his nose, you need to make it narrower, maybe I can help, I'm good at drawing, no, I haven't studied identikit drawing, but I'm an architect, his nose wasn't so wide, it was narrower, yes, that's it, now it's starting to look like him.

José went in a car with two plainclothes policemen. I went in another with the detective and a muscular man covered in tattoos. The vehicle I was in drove slowly, up the same road that a few days earlier I had travelled up on foot, clothed and intact, and on the way down, torn and broken. It was unbelievable that a simple run before a meeting now obliged me to retrace the route in a police car — civil police, but police nonetheless — trying to identify the exact place where the gloved hands had wrenched me from normality.

I felt like I was in a movie, the victim who exists merely to raise the suspense so that the hero can hunt for the clues that will eventually reward the victim, coming full circle, giving meaning to the initial despair, in this case my despair, the tears that returned as the car moved forward, and the hero, or in this case the heroine, the detective with hair down to her waist, asked me: Was it here?

Not yet, I said, not yet.

Supposedly, there is earnestness on the part of the police. A woman leads the case to foster identification and make me relax. They always ask permission to speak, to come in, and in this manner they keep asking, keep coming in, and before I know it I'm in the car with them. Everything begins to strike me as glaring and obvious, I find myself even more unprotected, I really want to throw myself onto my bed where, alone, I feel less helpless than I do with these police officers beside me. Nothing works, obviously, the earnestness doesn't work, the realism in excess makes everything unreal, trust me to agree to go ahead with this investigation, we're in Rio de Janeiro, Brazil, not a Hollywood movie, here there are only loose ends, rough edges, everything's such a mess that nothing works, there's no way it can work.

I knew how to identify the exact location, because on the way up to Vista Chinesa there's an emblematic place, a wall covered in graffiti known as the Wall of Relief, because it's where the slope becomes less steep and Vista Chinesa is near. Another kilometre and you can already see it. I liked running past this wall, because the graffiti is colourful and creates an optical illusion. The colours get into your head and mix with your thoughts, the music, and the endorphins. A man and woman kissing, a giant mushroom, a psychedelic tree, a whale, a mouth smoking a joint. Whoever drew those things must have been really high: a whale in the middle of the forest, a blue whale, everything so colourful, red, orange, purple, really vivid, eye-catching colours, unlike the forest, which is just green.

It was when the wall ended that the cold metal touched my temple, the blue or black small, medium, or large glove grabbed my arm. I remember seeing the end of the wall, perhaps the man even collided with the wall, perhaps he staggered as he collided with the wall, and me with him. Like in that 4D game that you kids love, the images combining with reality, fiction interacting with what's real, without your body being able to distinguish the spaces, the stranger dragged me away forcefully, saying incomprehensible words.

The Wall of Relief is on a bend, I said. It was at that bend. As soon as I pointed at the place, I felt the nausea coming on and asked to be taken home.

The detective came with me, asked if I was well, and asked for a glass of water. It was hot, that muggy, humid heat, the city's typical sultriness. The men stayed in the forest, the police officers and my brother. For three hours they scoured the forest, looked for vestiges among dry leaves, branches, almost identical trees, scoured the ground, the soil, the mud. Maybe a monkey, a toucan, or a five-metre-long boa constrictor weighing forty kilos had eaten the traces left there, the traces that they were looking for, a piece of his clothing, a piece of his glove, a strand of hair, but all they found were my trainers, the trainers I thought he'd taken to delay my encounter with the asphalt: wait fifteen minutes and go, and I felt the weight of the cold gun the entire time, the minutes or hours that I spent lost in the forest, before feeling my bare feet on the soft asphalt once again.

The calibre of the revolver, 38, 82, 85, 86, 88, 444, 608, the size of the revolver, small or large, the colour of the revolver, black or grey, new or used, and do you think I know anything about revolvers? Revolvers are revolvers to me, they're all revolvers, I wouldn't have a clue about the calibre, I've never touched a revolver, I've never felt a revolver. If I show you some images, can you identify it? Maybe. So then look at these. I looked, I swear I looked, and even those images were still just revolvers to me, a bunch of revolvers. All I can say is that it wasn't this one. The 608? Yes, the 608, the barrel wasn't that long, I remember his hand touching my head together with the revolver, so the barrel must have been short. I'm sorry, I told you I'm tired, I can't think straight, yes, I'm trying, I remember properly, it's you who's saying I don't remember, but I remember everything, or almost everything, but a revolver to me is just a revolver, there's just one name. Did you know the Eskimos have several words for the colour 'white', because each kind of white is a different colour to them, but we only have one, don't we? We call all the different whites 'white'— well, it's the same thing.

I awoke to the voices of the police officers in my apartment. By then, whatever was mine was ceasing to be mine. First, my body, then my apartment, people coming and going. Sometimes they didn't even call on the interphone, Severino would let them in, and suddenly I'd be woken by the doorbell. And I'd always be in a state of lethargy, because I was taking more tranquilisers than Dr Brito had recommended. Before, I used to brag about being so controlled, an organised, disciplined architect. I knew my thoughts by day, my thoughts by night, but out of the blue I began to hear voices, forest animals, the wind in the treetops, my bare feet on the leaves.

I'd fallen asleep in the armchair; my neck hurt. I remember seeing my trainers wrapped in plastic on the coffee table. And I remember feeling José's hand on my head, stroking it. Grandma's necklace, I asked, did you find it? José shook his head, then reassured me, Mum's on her way over.

A few minutes later she walked in, carrying a cake. She mustn't have imagined she would find so many people there, as she could barely hide her surprise. At the time I lived in a small one-bedroom apartment with a narrow living area ending in an open kitchen. The three police officers and detective were standing there, talking. My mother placed the plate on the counter, lifted up the cover, and asked, Would anyone like a piece?

The atmosphere was relaxed, each with their piece of cake, that *formigueiro* sponge cake with the chocolate sprinkles that my mother used to make when I was a kid and now makes for you kids and you love it, the cake I've never been able to eat since, but which was the only thing I could hold down then, my mother's cake, warm; if it was cold I'd put it in the microwave, to comfort me.

They were all entertained — including my mother, who was describing the secret to making it fluffy, and José, who was making coffee to go with the officers' snack — and no one noticed when I headed for the bathroom. I turned on the shower so I wouldn't hear the voices coming from the living room, and sat down with my face in my hands. To them, it was a case, it was work, they were having a coffee and a piece of cake on a break, as I did at the office when I was tired of drafting, when my eyes stung because of the light from the computer.

They were just living out their routine, hence a pause for a coffee, a trivial conversation; the voice raised to tell a funny story and a guffaw were absolutely normal. But my routine, my triviality, were suspended. I didn't want a bunch of people in my apartment; I didn't want to see the officers who were investigating the crime I was a victim of eating my mother's cake.

After knocking loudly on the door, José came into the bathroom and narrowed his eyes, waving away the steam with his arms. I lifted my head, our eyes met, and he asked, Are you OK? I hated answering that question, I hated hearing it, but knowing that the officers had left brought me a little peace, and lying on my bed between José and my mother, finally eating my piece of warm cake, made me think that even when nothing is OK there are moments when everything is OK.

I've brought images of several types of noses, said the forensic sketch artist as he spread laminated pages across the table:

The Nubian nose has a long, flat bridge with a downward-pointing tip.

The Greek nose is narrow and straight.

The hook nose is beak-like and curves downwards from the base to the tip.

The arched nose is like the hook nose, but has a slightly upturned tip.

The button nose is small and dainty.

The straight nose is flatter, with wide nostrils and a round tip.

The concave nose is small with a slight bump on the bridge.

The crooked nose has a bent bridge and rounded tip.

Could you point to the one that is closest to the nose of the man in question?

This business of calling the detective 'detective' was bothering me; I thought she was too important not to have a name, so I asked your father if he remembered the name of the detective who used to visit me at the apartment I lived in before we got married, before you came along, and he said, I think it was Gilda. It wasn't Gilda for sure, Gilda's my aunt's name. Oh, that's right, he said, if it wasn't Gilda, it was, it was … Regina? Gabriela? Wait, I've got it, Do, Du, Dulcineia! That's it, I shouted, Dulcineia! He wanted to know why I was asking, and I said I was writing about it, and he said, But you don't write, and I replied, It's just a letter, and he asked, A letter to who?, and I replied, To our children, and he said, But why do you like rummaging through the past so much?, and I said I wasn't rummaging through the past, I was rummaging through the present.

Come to think of it, it isn't really a letter. It's more of a testimony. No, not a testimony. A testament. The testament I don't want to leave you.

When I was pregnant, all I saw was pregnant women in the street, as if suddenly all women had decided to have children. They would pass me, smile, I'd smile back, and immediately afterwards I'd feel envious of their smiles, sincere smiles; after all, they loved being pregnant, carrying a being inside themselves, their hair was gorgeous, their skin was beautiful, their happiness could be seen in their eyes, and I, who had two babies, a boy and a girl, and I, who finally had everything I wanted, hated being pregnant. That is, I liked the idea. Sometimes, lying in bed, I would run my hand over my belly and was moved. But that business of carrying two babies around in my belly, nothing could have seemed more archaic, more bungling, more stupid on the part of nature. We learn at school that mammals are evolved, but I think it's the oviparous animals who are evolved. They lay a few eggs, and soon their offspring are born: they don't need to wait nine months, they don't have back pain, their skin doesn't get blotchy, they don't have constipation, insomnia, nightmares, shortness of breath, nausea, heartburn, tiredness, so much tiredness that I could fall asleep anywhere, in front of the computer, at the bar, I could even sleep while walking, and I had to explain myself, justify myself, because there are so many pregnant women out there who do everything normally, they work, sleep, dance, there are so many pregnant women out there full of life, who don't even bother to use the priority queue at the bank or the supermarket. On social media it was the same; suddenly, everyone was pregnant, but I think there's an explanation for it: all you have to do is search for nappies, a cot, or a pram on Google, and suddenly the only thing you see are photos of pregnant women and babies. Beautiful pregnant women, with make-up, half-naked, photoshopped by the best celebrity photographers, with no blemishes, no stretchmarks, their hair strong, healthy. I looked at myself in the mirror and said, I'm not like that, I'm not a pregnant woman like all the others, maybe these blemishes are my body's marks. I thought, The marks that stand out now, maybe pregnancy won't let me hide anything, but, no, I'm reading too much into it, it's in the books, these blemishes are common, so are the stretch marks, the tiredness, it just doesn't happen to all women, but it did with you.

I turned to Michel and said, I've made an appointment with a photographer. I thought he'd hate the idea, he hates that kind of photography, but I told him, The photographer is an artist, he assured me he wouldn't do one of those ridiculous albums, and, unexpectedly, Michel agreed, he even smiled, he seemed to like the idea. Off we went early one morning to the Tijuca Forest, and suddenly Michel pulled two fierce animal masks out of his backpack, handed me one and put the other one on, the photographer exclaimed, Brilliant!, and we took wild animals photos, which was how I actually felt, anything but human, and when the photos arrived it was the most beautiful thing I'd ever seen, my heart was filled with genuine emotion, an encounter with a lost identity, growing with each photo that I uploaded to Facebook and Instagram, the comments flooding in, wow, how powerful, you look gorgeous, pregnancy suits you, lots of heart emojis, pregnant and masked, pregnant and wild, pregnant and animalistic, and suddenly I was pregnant and happy, pregnant and ridiculously happy, I'd never felt so beautiful, so adapted to my body, how wonderful it was to be pregnant, with twins to boot, a joy.

Those are the masks you kids love playing with. The two of you as wild animals running through the house, screeching and roaring, using the same masks that Mummy and Daddy wore for photos in Tijuca Forest, now hanging in your room.

I did an internet search, and found the same nose drawings that the sketch artist had shown me. Beside them was a subjective description of the owners of each shape:

Nubian nose: Curious and optimistic, Nubian nose owners try to please others. They seek solutions for every problem.

Greek nose: Practical and loyal, people with Greek noses find it hard to talk about their feelings. They can seem aloof.

Hook nose: Fervent defenders of their beliefs, these people aren't averse to risk-taking in order to attain their goals.

Arched nose: People with arched noses love their work and are highly organised.

Button nose: Button nose owners are spontaneous decision-makers, which can be trying for others.
Straight nose: Straight-nosed people tend to have strong personalities and get angry quickly.
Concave nose: Generous and always ready to help others. These people are also sensitive and easily offended.
Crooked nose: Good listeners and down to earth, crooked-nosed people make great friends and partners.

Now: which nose is most like that of the man in question?

I overheard one of the policemen whisper to Michel that before the guy was officially arrested, before he was tried, he would have to reckon with him, Michel. The officer understood that Michel had the right to settle the score with the man who had defiled the purity of his woman's body. A man-to-man thing. Michel could do what he wanted with him — punch him in the face, pull out his teeth, kick him in the balls. The law was weak, very weak, it was lenient on perpetrators, and the police were there to ensure that the law of man was fulfilled, the law of instinct, not that ridiculous paper law.

Michel didn't say anything to me, nor I to him. I have no idea what was going through his head, if he wanted to be alone with the man or not, but that afternoon I couldn't think of anything else. What would I do if the officer told me: Now you can do whatever you want, use his body as you wish, we just need him alive, because he needs to be arrested, the newspapers need to show him in custody, our duty fulfilled, apart from that you can do as you wish. Punch him? Kick him? Scratch him? OK to set him on fire? Poke him in the eye? What would I do if he was in front of me again, this time in handcuffs, and I alone with him in a room where the police could come and save me at any moment, and safe, at the police station, not in the forest, just the two of us again, but me being able to do whatever I wanted to him now? I told myself: I'm against the death sentence, I don't believe in an eye for an eye, a tooth for a tooth, I can't think these things, I can't want to beat him up, kill him, cut off his dick so he'll never do it to any woman ever again, so he'll never stick his dick anywhere else ever again, so he'll never feel pleasure again, I can't think that I'd like to get a chainsaw and cut off his dick, his body mutilated forever, like mine.

The land where the Olympic golf course was being built had been, decades earlier, an Integrated Public Education Centre factory. The prefabricated structures that were made there were taken to other sites all over the city and put together, piece by piece, until the buildings were finished, whole. But that was a long time ago, when Brizola was governor.

The owner of the land was a magnate; much of the land on which the neighbourhood of Barra da Tijuca sat was his. After accusations by environmentalists, the Rio de Janeiro attorney-general's office launched an inquiry into excessive profits in the construction of the Olympic golf course. The document said there was a flagrant disproportion between what the owner was earning and what the city was losing or failing to earn.

Environmentalists alleged that, in addition to being an environmental crime, the construction companies would have exaggerated gains because the cost of building the course was somewhere in the vicinity of sixty million reais, while the potential for profit was as much as one billion reais.

In the beginning, it was just the smell. His smell, the smell of jack fruit, a smell that comes to me to this day in the most unexpected places — on holiday in Mexico, sipping margaritas by the sea, suddenly it's there, the same smell that I smelled walking through the forest. I don't choose it, it comes when it wants to, where it wants to. If someone were to say now: Remember the smell, I wouldn't be able to. It decides when it wants to be remembered. It's different from someone saying, Remember the guy, and I remember him.

I noticed a strange tone of voice when Dulcineia asked me why I'd gone for a run in the afternoon if I always went in the morning. I don't know if I was getting paranoid — police, you know how it is, who trusts the police in Rio de Janeiro? — but suddenly she was insisting, Why did you go for a run in the afternoon if you always go in the morning?, as if the key to the crime might be in my answer. I was going to work out, I said, and I saw curiosity, surprise, in her eyes. If you were going to work out, why did you go for a run to Vista Chinesa? The meeting, I replied, the time of the meeting changed, it was brought forward, and Cadu ... Who's Cadu? Cadu called me at the last minute, I was on my way out, I had to come back, it would have been impossible to go to the gym. Is it that far away? It's in Gávea. By the time I'd got the car, parked, worked out, showered, come home, there might have been traffic, it would've been risky. Risky?, Dulcineia asked, her tone of voice ironic. She must think I don't want to collaborate, I thought, after all, the gloves are thin then thick, blue then black, the nose is small then large, and I kept on rejecting all of the photographs of suspects, but the tone of the question, that almost incriminating question, Why did you go for a run in the afternoon if you always go in the morning?, didn't sit well with me. Yes, I knew it was more dangerous in the afternoon, but I'd looked through the window, seen the sun shining through the trees, and thought there wouldn't be a problem. You thought there wouldn't be a problem? That's right, I answered, already annoyed. But there was a problem, she said. Yep, I agreed, there was. And that was when I convinced myself that the next time she showed me a photo of a suspect, I would agree to see him, maybe she was right, maybe it was better to see him live, it wasn't always possible to recognise someone in a photograph like that, and they had much more experience than me, they worked with crimes, suspects, victims, felons, I was complicating things, I wasn't cooperating, but I will cooperate, I told myself that instant, before she said goodbye and shut the door to my apartment.

That night, my mother burst into the living room, tossed her bag on the sofa, and hugged me. I was groggy, the effect of the meds I'd taken after the detective's visit, and I felt nauseated from the cocktail, a nausea that blended with my nausea of the memory of what had happened, my body limp, unable to support itself, a body that was decomposing, that I wanted to disappear. She hugged me hard, as if, unlike me, she wanted the concreteness of my body, the solidity of my athlete's muscles, her strong, healthy daughter, the daughter who never stopped, the daughter who enjoyed the city without fear, she wanted me as I was before, intact, and the longer she hugged me the more certain I was that she'd never have that daughter back again. Not the way I used to be. A piece of me, a big piece of me had remained in the forest, lost, torn, scraps of flesh, food for the animals.

———

If I was alone with the stranger in a room of the police station, with him handcuffed in front of me, I'd clobber him, I'd beat him until his face was deformed and no one would ever recognise him again, not even my memory. If I was alone with the stranger in a room of the police station, I'd hack at him with a knife, his guts spilling out, the floor covered in blood, his voice agonising slowly until his last breath. Before that, his dick dangling, no, his dick cut off and stuffed in his mouth so I wouldn't have to hear his cries. But I didn't say it. Nor did I imagine it.

The first time I was naked in front of Michel after the rape, I thought: He's seeing the whole truth on my body. Now he knows, my body can't hide what I didn't tell him. I covered myself, he put his arms around me, told me to be patient, because with time everything would fall back into place. We're not in a hurry, he said.

The second time I was naked in front of Michel, I thought the same thing. I took longer to cover myself, but I did. The third time, the fourth, the fifth, always the same feeling, and Michel always telling me that he wasn't in a hurry. But not me, and I slowly trained myself, forcing myself to give more and more, thinking: One day it will pass, one day I'll take off my clothes and I won't think that he can see I was violated.

I'm not bothered about the scar from the c-section. The crooked line and the keloid don't change my idea of perfection, but that Tuesday in the forest is not only riveted in my soul, as I thought would happen. It's also stamped across my body. Everything is written on my skin, I know it is, everything that happened, even the details I said I'd told the police but didn't tell them because you can never tell it all, there's always something missing.

That Tuesday impacted my physical appearance as if my body could never again be the same body for which I was willing to run up to Vista Chinesa and down again. There are days when I think it will pass, I won't feel the same discomfort in front of the mirror, I'll be attractive again, I'll enjoy showing my body again, because, as your father said, it's a matter of patience after all.

The artist held out the sketch. I took a step back, sat on the sofa, breathless. Dulcineia brought me a glass of water, I began to breathe again, I took the paper, the finished sketch, the man, the stranger in front of me, yes, it was him, very similar, almost the same, maybe the face was a little rounder than his, maybe the mouth was a little thinner, but, yes, it was him, after hours of answering the artist's questions, finally there was the sketch, in front of me, there was the man, the stranger, except on paper. It'll be easier with this, said Dulcineia, we'll catch him. It'd be better if you hadn't showered, but a well-drawn identikit sketch is a big help. We'll catch the guy, trust me, you'll see him behind bars, she said, the desire for revenge leaping out of her eyes. And there's more: my men went back to the forest, they found your necklace, it's been sent off for analysis, we're hoping to find a clue that will lead us to your attacker, I'll keep you posted. My grandma's necklace, I exclaimed, caught between the relief of knowing they'd found it and the distress of knowing it wasn't there, that it had been sent to the police station without my consent.

The identikit sketch was published in the newspaper the next day with a summary of the story. They didn't print my name, but they did say that the victim was working on a project for the 2016 Rio Olympics. I stared at the picture until the image blurred, lost its contours, and dissipated. It was a game I used to play at the time: I'd half-close my eyes and concentrate on any old object until it dissolved. I did it with the man, the stranger, and he became little white balls scattered in the air.

Six months after the rape, I still wasn't well. Time didn't alleviate the pain, which was insistent from the second I opened my eyes, when the morning light came through the cracks in the window and the birds sang in the trees in the street. Then Michel suggested we take a trip. We could go to a beach in Bahia, maybe Boipeba or Caraíva — I could choose, and he'd take care of the details. I held his hands, smiled with a certain indulgence. His gesture moved me, although I was certain that no paradisiacal beach could take away the affliction that consumed me daily.

A week later, I told him I wanted to go to Mexico. I'd wanted to go ever since the death of my grandmother, who always used to tell me about the time she'd lived there, a long time ago. I agreed that the city of Mexico wasn't the ideal place for a break. I proposed Tulum, Caribbean beaches, and Mayan constructions. Sun and ruins. His eyes smiled, and he quickly set about organising the trip. In those days, the people around me would try to propose goals to me, find purpose in something nearby so that I would want to move forward. Each time someone thought they had found my salvation, I could see the smile in their eyes. And that was my goal, the sense of purpose that stopped me sinking into the sofa, while the city of Rio de Janeiro rebuilt itself for something grandiose.

We went in search of the cliché — beautiful, exotic beaches for a new beginning — because in sadness and the desire to return to life no one wonders if they are doing the obvious. We flew to Cancun, where we hired a car and drove to Tulum. Along the way, Michel and I would sometimes look at one another in silence, hoping terribly that the plan would work, and terribly afraid that it wouldn't.

The hotel gate was the most unexpected thing I'd ever seen. An enormous indigenous figure made of wood, with painted skin, tore its own chest open with its hands. As if we were invading its body, we entered through a dirt road lined with plants. Continuing on, we came to reception. A relief, almost joy, gripped me as I listened to the young man behind the counter, his skin very dark, his hair straight and black, a friendliness that we encountered everywhere: He doesn't know a thing, I thought. He doesn't know who I am, who I've become. He doesn't know what happened to me. No one here knows.

With this feeling of freedom I headed to our bungalow, an isolated cabin on the sand, with tree trunks at the entrance, a thatched roof, and rustic decoration; in the centre, a bed with a mosquito net around it. Around the bungalow, a tropical infinity of trees and plants. Out front, a crystal-blue sea. A setting conceived in such a way that everything in it worked, discreet architecture embedded in nature, the sound of the waves, the clear sky.

On the bed was a menu of everything the hotel had to offer, from massages and local purification baths to yoga classes and hikes, in a mixture of Mexico and India. I looked at my watch: the meditation session was in little over an hour. I thought it would be a good way to get into the atmosphere of the trip. Michel preferred to rest.

At the front door were two large wooden elephants. At the back of the small room, which smelled of incense, was an altar replete with Indian figurines. In the rest of the space, eight rugs lay side by side, only two of them empty. I sat on one and smiled at the instructor, who smiled back, while the other people sat there with their eyes closed, one hand over the other, palms facing upwards, in a meditation mudra. I copied the posture, and the instructor began to direct our breathing: first, abdominal; then the air rises, opening up the ribs and chest. When your mind flits off, bring it back to the breathing, she said.

My mind flits off and I breathe, my mind flits off and I breathe. With our hands on our chests, we repeat 'Om' three times, and then the instructor asks us to open our eyes and explains that we're going to spend the next twenty minutes repeating a mantra. If anyone feels uncomfortable in the lotus position, they can get a cushion or block. Her voice leads the process: Let your thoughts pass, don't latch on to any image. No one can keep an empty mind; an empty mind is thoughts passing like a train that never stops, just passes by. If you realise you're stuck on an image, focus on your breathing.

The more I try to focus on my breathing, the more the image stagnates there, the same image, the static thought. I repeat the mantra, think about my breathing, but the image won't leave, the train stopped at the station. I don't know how to meditate. I open my eyes and see everyone else with their eyes closed allowing the images to slide by; I close my eyes again, and the image is still there. Is it me or the image that's in charge, is it me or the image that decides what to remember, is the memory mine or is it an independent being that parks itself there even when I'm trying to meditate? I breathe, first in my belly, then my ribs, then my chest, but the image doesn't leave. I open and close my eyes, and there it is, and suddenly out comes a sob, loud, uncontrollable, it leaves my throat before I have time to stop it, it comes once, twice, three times in a row, and slowly one, two, three people open their eyes and turn to me. I try not to look at them, until one of them decides to get up and wrap her arms around me, and then another, the whole room, people I don't know, tourists who have come to unwind in the transparent blue Caribbean sea all hugging me at the same time, and I am deeply sorry that I sobbed, that I'm in that state. I don't want to embrace people I don't know. I want to get up and go back to my room. I close myself in a cocoon, hugging my legs, and the people start to get up and move back to their own rugs. I lie on the ground, close my eyes, and the image is no longer there. Now I see the house I lived in as a child.

I was at the office when Dulcineia's assistant called me saying, We have a guy here at the police station in Campo Grande who looks like the guy in the identikit sketch. I'm going to send you a photo, and you tell me if I can have him transferred to Gávea.

I shook in the minutes that followed. The file didn't arrive, I went to the window to see if it was a problem with the signal, then my phone pinged. Looking at the photograph, I stammered, It isn't him. I enlarged it to see it more closely. Come to think of it, there were similarities. Maybe it was my attacker. I closed and opened my eyes, as Dulcineia had told me to do: it was him, it wasn't him. Before that, I was certain I'd recognise him. But right then and there, I wasn't sure of anything. In two weeks, he might have changed, made some changes to throw off the police. In two weeks, certainty might have become doubt, the days might have blurred the contours I had in my mind. Besides which, a photograph is just a photograph. The smell of rotten jack fruit came to me, the smell of the forest, the smell of the man, my stomach knotting up. I made it to the bathroom in time to vomit. Looking in the mirror I thought: I don't even recognise myself.

When I returned to the living room, the phone was ringing. So, can I send him over? The officer sounded serious and in a hurry. Yes, I replied drily. Is it him? I don't know, maybe, I need to see him.

At five o'clock, I was there. Diana arrived right after me. I filled out the usual paperwork, that incomprehensible bureaucracy, and waited for them to call me. Diana waited for me outside.

Dulcineia saw me in the corridor and gave me a kiss on each cheek, friendly. We got the guy, she said with an enormous smile. I was taken to a room and placed in front of a window through which I could see an empty room. Suddenly the door opened, and five men walked into the room and formed a line. I opened my eyes wide and recognised the one from the photograph. The others looked nothing like him. Who are they all?, I asked the assistant. We always bring more than one so as not to induce the victim. But ... I was going to say, but just thought it: How so, if they've already sent me a photograph of the suspect?

They made each one state his name and profession so I could hear their voices, but they became jumbled in my head, I could barely distinguish them from one another, they were confusing echoes that meant nothing to me, and I asked them to speak a little more, so each man added his age and the name of the neighbourhood he lived in. I concentrated on the suspect's voice, which didn't sound like the stranger's voice but sounded different with each sentence. I couldn't pin it down, it was mobile, soluble.

The officer asked if there was anyone I wanted to dismiss, anyone I was sure wasn't the suspect. I looked again at the men, and suddenly they began to confuse me. While previously I'd thought it wasn't any of them, now I was certain it was all of them. Mouths, noses, ears, eyes, skin colour, hair texture, everything combining and becoming a single person, the same rapist. I felt dizzy, the voice of the assistant asking insistently, Well?, my inability to give an answer, the noses growing longer, becoming crooked, mouths widening, ears retracting, the eyes of one on the face of another, the hands of one on the arms of another, on the legs of another, a futuristic painting, until finally my voice said, No, I don't want to dismiss anyone. Then his voice was interrogative, pressing me, Why not? You need to choose the ones who look the most like him. They all do, I replied, they all look like him. It was them, I said. No, I didn't say it, but I thought it.

In disbelief he looked at me and asked, Do you need help? I went quiet for a moment; did that police officer really think he could help by placing five culprits in front of me? I was alternating between lucidity and madness, calm and nervousness, common sense and anxiety, when, in reticence, I ended up choosing two.

Pointing at the man in the photograph, the assistant asked, Is it him? It is, isn't it? Just like the sketch. Don't forget that sometimes we think the nose is like this when it's really like that. Imitating Dulcineia, he repeated, open and close your eyes. Take a good look. Have a good think.

I opened and closed my eyes several times. Was it him or wasn't it? Was it?

In Dulcineia's office, she asked, The verdict? I hesitated. I choked. She continued, a little disappointed, So? I replied, I don't think so. You don't?! I don't. I mean, it isn't him. He has some similar features, but it isn't him. His voice is too different. His body. He's taller. The face is similar in one or two aspects, but it isn't him.

Dulcineia stood, clearly annoyed, her eyes trained on mine. Júlia, I'm going to explain something to you: you have experienced trauma. Trauma, understand? You can't think you remember everything ... I'm going to change the question. I don't want you to tell me if it's him or not him anymore, I want you to tell me: does he look like the guy?

I didn't answer.

She went on: Do the suspect's eyes look like the eyes of the man who attacked you?

No.

Why not?

They're smaller.

What about the colour?

The colour, I think so. But almost everyone has brown eyes, don't they?

Does the suspect's nose look like the nose of the man who attacked you?

I think so.

Stop thinking so. Does it?

A little.

How so?

The triangular shape.

Does the suspect's mouth look like the mouth of the man who attacked you?

A little, too.

How so?

Both are thin-lipped, but the guy's was even more so.

More so how?

Thinner lips. Less fleshy.

Does the suspect's colour look like the colour of the man who attacked you?

Yes.

Explain.

They both have a kind of olive complexion, like me but a bit lighter.

Do you have anything to add?

I don't think so.

Then you can go.

Diana was waiting for me outside. She wanted to know every detail. I told her a little, then changed the subject. We strolled down to Leblon Beach, the sky almost dark, a few silver clouds behind the sea. The waves were crashing hard on the sand. Rio's beautiful, I sighed, as if beauty could save us, myself and the city. So are you, I heard Diana say, you're beautiful, too. I held her hand, and we continued walking and talking until we came to Jardim de Alah Park.

From the day we'd met, that hand had held mine so many times. Diana knew how to respect my silence and bring up topics that lifted me up without seeming like she was going out of her way to be nice to me. A discreet way to show that pain accompanies us, but that what matters is being alive, feeling alive.

Staring at the ceiling with Márcia behind me, I said, it all started when I was learning to read and write. I was the last one in my class to learn to read. I couldn't repeat the syllables, pay attention to a text from start to finish — my mind would drift off. The teacher had each student read a book aloud, and I was the only one who couldn't do it. I asked my mother to read me *Mico Maneco* over and over until I memorised it. The next day at school, I told the story perfectly, but my sentences didn't match the pages. The teacher called my parents and arranged to meet them. I think your daughter has dyslexia. She confuses the letters 'f' and 'v,' 'm' and 'n,' and she has a hard time concentrating on reading. From the school I was sent to a paediatrician, a neuropsychologist, a speech therapist; my parents were determined to save me. Our house filled up with post-its with the letters 'f' and 'v.' I had to repeat the sounds, 'ffff,' 'vvvv.'

At the age of eleven, I joined the Book Circle to learn to concentrate. By this time, I rarely got my letters mixed up, but my perception of the passage of time was irregular; I didn't understand the idea of sequence very well, the way things follow one another. Interrupting a book before the end distressed me, but things didn't seem to happen in any order, I had to go back to the beginning to remember what I'd read, and I ended up getting lost. So I took my new activity seriously: every day I had to read just one passage of a book or a newspaper article, summarise it, and tell my fellow classmates what it was about.

Dyslexics are more sensitive, my parents said. While they're not advancing in language, they're honing the part of the brain responsible for intuition. Einstein, Da Vinci, Mozart, and Agatha Christie were also dyslexics, and I didn't want to let my parents down; I decided that I was going to be an excellent student, and studied like mad. I made study cards for everything, wrote out the same word hundreds of times, and that was when I understood that obsession bears fruit. And people who are obsessive know how easy it is to go from one obsession to the next.

I was seventeen when I decided that I was going to have a beautiful body, and a beautiful body meant being thin, very thin. The less I ate, the more I worked out, the thinner I'd be, closer to perfection. Yes, a beauty standard was just a convention, but it had been established that in this century an attractive woman was a thin woman, and I didn't want to be fat, just as I didn't want to be bottom of the class in Portuguese. The pleasure I felt getting a test back with praise from my teacher was the same as the pleasure of looking at myself naked in the mirror and not seeing a tummy or cellulite, the pleasure of wearing a short dress, tight clothing, going to the beach in Ipanema and being able to show off my body.

And now, how long has it been? I keep on working out, running, doing krav maga, but every time I see myself naked in the mirror I see my attacker, and he tells me there's no point trying, my body's been shattered, and a shattered body will never be a beautiful body.

When I stopped talking, Márcia asked, Is that what you think? After a few seconds of silence, I said, The ceiling's cracking. Look, there's an enormous crack. Have you noticed? Maybe you should call a painter.

The sea in Tulum is transparent blue. It doesn't appear to have any thickness to it. It doesn't look like the portal to a deep, mysterious kingdom. You look down and see the fish, the corals, the squid, you see your feet and the feet of the other beachgoers. Even when dark clouds cover the sky, even when a storm breaks, the sea in Tulum remains transparent blue.

Michel and I were in the water when my gaze paused on something in the distance, on the horizon, and I saw the water pull back. Nowadays everyone knows that when the water pulls back it's because a giant wave, a tsunami, will follow it, like the one that devastated the island of Phuket in 2004 and killed more than 230,000 people. The water's pulling back, I said, let's get out of here. No, my love, it's your eyes, it's in the same place, I heard Michel say. Did you know that in Thailand a child saved a bunch of people because they'd just learned at school that when the water pulls back, a giant wave comes, a wave that swallows everything, drags everything away? Together with the child, hundreds of people fled to a mountaintop and didn't die. If we stay here, waiting to see the birth of the giant wave, we'll die. Michel didn't say anything. Fear was growing inside me, the sea was pulling back, and Michel just stood there as if it were nothing. Then I screamed, Tsunami, tsunami!, and suddenly I felt Michel's hands grab me, drag me away, I felt his arms around me, I kicked him, tried to break free, he wouldn't let go, we were wasting time, Let's go, let's run. He held me so tightly I couldn't move, so I closed my eyes; I preferred to be swallowed without seeing it.

The broad tree supported him, his short, strong body against the hard trunk. The hand pulling my hair took me to the most terrible place, while I thought, Please, not that, but no thought could stop him from doing whatever he wanted, and that was when I began telling myself that it was best not to think, I didn't want to resist because I'd read, I'd heard somewhere that in rape the more you resist, the more the rapist likes it; if you're quiet and accept it, you might be lucky, and he might not like it and leave; if you pretend you're enjoying it, your chances are better; but I didn't know how to be quiet, I didn't know how to obey and open my mouth as he was ordering me to, when my face reached his dick. Then he tugged hard on my hair and pushed against my mouth, which stayed closed until his rough hands forced my jaw open, causing me to smell and taste what I didn't want to, the smell and taste that come back to me together with the smell and taste of jackfruit, his dick rubbing against my teeth, me trying to hide my tongue in some corner of my mouth so I wouldn't taste it, trying not to breathe so I wouldn't smell it. I thought again that if I tried, I could pretend I was enjoying it, but what overcame me was the urge to bite off his dick, spit his dick out in the forest; what I felt was fury, a deep loathing, an urge to be crueller to him than he was being to me, but also an urge to vomit, shortness of breath, my eyes closed, dizziness, my mind losing control, allowing itself to drift, as if it was the only way I could not go crazy there, that very instant, as if it was the only way I could not die there, that very instant.

Three days after my visit to the police station, it was Dulcineia herself who called me. So, do you have an answer? I felt lost. An answer to what? I can't hold the man for much longer, she said. The man? Hold? Had the suspect been at the police station since my visit? I lost my balance, the phone slipped out of my hand, and I heard Dulcineia talking on the other end. My voice faltering, I said, I didn't know… Can you come here now? Her voice was incisive. I was at work and had to finish a lateral section of the golf course by the next day. I didn't want there to be any flaws.

But the man was being held because I couldn't tell if he was guilty or not. I left the office in a hurry.

The same room with a window and the man there, unable to see me as I observed him. This time, I didn't close my eyes. I left them open for a long time, I listened to his voice again, I examined every detail of his body, his face, I concentrated on the way he moved, talked, breathed. I was shaking constantly, my heart racing, a bitter taste in my mouth, nausea. It was in my hands to decide if that man was going to go home or be arrested. And, in prison, treated like a rapist, beaten, attacked, probably raped himself. I want to be left alone, I told the assistant.

On my way to Dulcineia's office, I formulated what I was going to say. I had to be very careful with my words. I couldn't hesitate, show any doubt.

No, I said.

Are you sure?

Her biased expression made me think for the first time that the police just wanted to arrest someone, it didn't matter who, what mattered was closing the case, saying in the newspapers that they'd found the guy, that I'd recognised him, it was him. I saw it on Dulcineia's face: she had no doubt he was the culprit, she was ready to see her conviction through to the end, she just needed me to say, It's him. And for an instant, looking at his face, I thought I could put a full stop to everything. I, and I alone, had the power to end that torment once and for all, to find peace for my family and for Dulcineia. In my answer, her glory.

Would I be able to live not only with the memory of the stranger tearing off my clothes and flogging me with a belt, but also with that of the other man, yes, the other man, who would go to jail with one word from me? That man might have a family, a job, he'd probably never done anything bad to anyone; he could be arrested, beaten, raped, if I accused him.

Yes, I said. I'm sure.

Dulcineia sighed heavily. You can go, then. I'll call you when we find another suspect. If we find one.

She emphasised the *If*, almost a threat, or a request for me to reconsider. It was just the two of us in the room; no one would know if I changed my mind. But I didn't. I went ahead with it, signed the papers, and left with a feeling of relief, a lightness that I hadn't felt in a long time. I didn't want just any man behind bars. I wanted it to be the stranger who'd pressed a cold gun to my forehead, who'd made me walk through the forest not knowing where I was going, pushing me to the ground and letting his pants down. Him, or no one. My peace of mind back.

At home, I looked at the identikit sketch again. The man at the police station was reminiscent of the man in the sketch, who in turn was reminiscent of the man who had raped me, but just how alike was he? I closed and opened my eyes over and over, trying to locate the differences. With my eyes closed, I concentrated on the image of the real man. I'd open my eyes and see the man on paper, another man, similar, the same, different. Why was it that every time I opened my eyes, the man in my head vanished? Why couldn't I hold onto that image?

I was born strange, a very ugly baby. As I grew, I became ungainly and buck-toothed, and my parents decided that I'd have to get braces. Back then, everyone who wore braces was teased at school. To make things worse, I was the only one with braces attached to headgear, and that was how my purgatory began. On the dance floors of teen discos in Rio's South Zone, I was the one nobody asked to dance. I'd dance with a broom — literally with a broom. Sometimes I'd be saved by Rafael Augusto, a boy with a heart problem whose lips and fingernails were always purple as a result. He suffered from the same problem as me, being different from everyone else at an age in which difference is anything but an advantage. Dyslexic, with headgear, and chubby, I felt like the worst of all creatures.

One sunny day, we were both in front of the school when three boys a year above us came and made fun of us, the cadaver and the donkey. Oh, what a cute couple, oh, woo-hoo, their guffaws coming through the gate. Rafael Augusto and I were tongue-tied, used to the joke, but tongue-tied. Other students going in, the gate closing, 7.40 a.m. Aren't you going in? No. What are you going to do? Want to go to the beach?

Rafael Augusto and I on the 583 bus on a Wednesday morning, backpacks on our laps, the silence, Rio's South Zone passing in the window, Laranjeiras, Botafogo, Humaitá, Jardim Botânico, Gávea, Leblon, Ipanema. We got off the bus and walked almost without speaking, only making a comment now and then about our maths and geography teachers.

The beach was empty, with just a few surfers in the water. I had a jumper tied around my waist, and that was what I sat on, my feet bare. Shyness raised a wall between us. I remember thinking that no one could see us there, no one could know I'd skipped class to go to the beach with him, the boy with a heart problem whose lips and fingernails were always purple as a result.

Rafael Augusto stood up and took off his T-shirt, his weak, curved body moving away, the sun beating on his back. When he saw me beside him with my school clothes drenched, he said I was crazy. How was I going to go home? I shrugged and sank underwater. The water was calm, the temperature perfect, and I didn't want to think about the future. I hadn't even remembered to leave my headgear in my backpack. I can still hear Rafael Augusto's voice saying, Take it off. And me holding the gear, swinging it back and forth, with a childish smile.

Suddenly, unexpectedly, my body was enveloped by a big wave, and my hair was full of sand. Where was the headgear? Another big wave. I dived under, quickly, my hand reaching for his under the water until I found it; this time, a deep dive, and the wave breaking above our bodies without dragging us along. Then another; they always come in threes.

Then the sea was calm again, the two of us looking for the headgear, me diving under repeatedly to try to get the sand out of my hair and clothes. My mother's going to kill me, I said, it cost a fortune. When we gave up, there it was, at the water's edge, rocking back and forth.

After allowing some time to pass, I started walking, lost in the forest, barefoot, afraid, it's getting dark, I thought, I need to get to the road quickly, I ran, walked, stopped, breathed, the light fading, the cicadas singing, a leaf, another leaf, another leaf, a mosquito, another mosquito, another mosquito, impossible to count the details in the tropical forest, running, walking barefoot, I couldn't feel my feet, suddenly I remembered the necklace, the necklace my grandma had brought from her years in Mexico, the necklace she'd always worn, the necklace with the pendant of the goddess Ixchel, the Mayan goddess, a woman with a serpent in her hair against a full moon, the necklace I'd inherited from my grandma, that my grandma had given me shortly before she died, which the rapist had yanked off my neck when he ordered me to lick his face and the necklace hit his chin, his fury at the necklace, hurling it away, me thinking at the time, If I survive I'm going to look for the necklace, but I'd forgotten that, and now I remembered, I thought about going back, but to where?, where had I come from?, where would I go?, darkness settling on the forest, and I didn't even feel the urge coming, but I felt, I can feel it now, the wee running down my legs, so much of it, I don't know why I wet my pants, I don't remember feeling the urge, or having a full bladder, I just remember the wee running down my legs, wetting my leggings already wet with sweat, with humidity, fear.

Today I told Márcia I'm writing this letter to you kids. Right at the beginning of the session, I said, I've started writing not knowing exactly what to say, how to say it, but certain that I can't keep quiet. Little by little, I've begun to realise that I don't remember everything.

After a while in which I said nothing, she murmured, Yes.

Don't think I've forgotten, I went on. I remember every day. Sometimes one detail; sometimes many. But every last thing, impossible. If I'd told someone every last detail at the time, if I'd written down each step, would my memory be any different? I don't know how much all those visits to the police station scrambled my head. Time, pregnancy, childbirth, and breastfeeding are also things that make you forget. It's like your brain focuses on survival and the joy of your children, and forgets almost everything else. For example, birthdays. I don't remember anyone's birthday anymore.

I don't want to avoid the subject. I left home today with the objective of telling the story. So many years have passed, and I'm still not free of it. I don't know if I ever will be. Will I?

I'm so afraid of passing it on to my children, I told Márcia.

Antonia's in the why phase now. The other day, a friend at school was sad because her dog had died, and Antonia wanted to know what death was. I explained it more or less, because you can't really explain death to a three-year-old child, and when I finished she asked me if I was going to die one day, and when I said, Yes, she asked, Why, Mummy? I was so moved, we hugged each other tightly, with so much tenderness, a love that I can't even describe, thinking, She's my continuity, just as I'm my mother's continuity, sometimes we're one and the same, we're the synthesis of this past-present-future contained in all three of us, a single person. I was caught up in this feeling, truly happy. It was a happy moment, until I realised: We can't be one and the same. We can't be the same person. Not even more or less the same person. I don't want my story to be my daughter's story, my body to be my daughter's body. Then that light, sweet happiness began to give way to fear, to anxiety. Guilt. With mothers, it's always guilt. I began to feel like I was to blame for having this ruined body, for not having resolved the problem to this day, for thinking about that Tuesday even when I was hugging my daughter. She didn't deserve it, doesn't deserve it. She has nothing to do with the story; she was conceived later, born later, but if we're one and the same, I thought, she'll end up feeling raped, too. The mother's rape reflected in her daughter's body. Then I looked at Antonia, and thought that maybe she would look in the mirror and feel ugly, feel a veiled violence in her skin. Her of all people, so beautiful, so pure.

I stopped talking, swallowed my tears, breathed.

I'm also worried about Martim. We've already been to several paediatricians, a child neurologist, a developmental paediatrician — the things they come up with — and I've already taken him to the psychoanalyst that you recommended. Everyone says he's normal, that he interacts, communicates, has a sense of humour, shows affection, is loving. But he's three years old and doesn't speak. He says a few bits of words, almost no whole ones, just 'Mummy,' 'Daddy,' 'wee wee,' 'poo poo,' and 'bread,' and the rest are just bits. He can mime like no one else. At day care, they say he's going to be an actor; he'll throw himself on the ground to make himself understood, he leads people to things, but he doesn't speak. Yes, I know boys take longer to speak than girls, but Antonia was already speaking at one and a half, and by the age of two she was a chatterbox, but Martim, nothing. Yes, I know children all have their own pace, that I shouldn't get anxious or show him that I want him to speak. Maybe he's dyslexic like me, but my speech wasn't delayed. The speech therapist told me that there are different kinds of dyslexia, and when I asked if there could be something emotional behind his refusal to speak, she snapped, He isn't refusing, it's hard for him. But I can't get it out of my head: Martim refuses to speak.

That's why I decided to write them a letter, I continued. Telling it in a way that I never have before. This idea of the details came to me. That perhaps the cure is in the details. It's the details that will free me of the whole. The precise position of every tree, the precise smell of every leaf, the precise number of steps we took in the forest, the stranger and me.

I went quiet. The white ceiling falling on my head.

But it'll be impossible. I don't remember everything precisely. No one ever remembers anything precisely, do they? Maybe if I were to tell it several times. If I talked about nothing else, if I only repeated the same story every day I came here, putting all of my versions together, maybe I'd get there. At some point, I'd get it all out and free myself of this past. I'd free Antonia and Martim of this past, because at the end of the day that's what matters.

I heard the sound of Márcia moving in the chair. She was going to get up, shake my hand and say, We'll continue. And that's what she did.

We returned to the bungalow after three margaritas at the beach bar. Stumbling, I went to the bathroom to take off my makeup, which was bothering me, the weight of the eyeliner on my eyelids. I lay on the bed and put my arms around Michel, my body somewhere between lethargy and the desire to turn the embrace into something else, my hands sliding over his back, then resting, to begin again. He leaned his head towards me and kissed me, a long, calm kiss, while his hand imitated mine, travelling very slowly over my back, my arm, putting off the moment in which he would reach my breast, all so slow and sweet, as if it were our first time in bed, and we, adolescents who didn't know how far to go. He didn't want to pass any limits, I realised, he was feeling his way, one thing at a time, afraid to hurt me. But suddenly his hands on my breasts were turning me on. I said, Harder. He pressed. I insisted, More. I put my hands over his and pressed down. I bit his lips, he moaned, I took off my blouse, my bra, I raised my breasts to his mouth, which was bleeding slightly. As he sucked on them, I said, Harder. I pulled off his clothes in a hurry and sat on him. I moved quickly, squeezing him inside me, while his hands squeezed my arse, and mine squeezed his nipples. Without me showing any sign of stopping, he said, wide-eyed, Don't stop, and then he gripped me hard and came. I lay down beside him feeling a joy greater than the joy of an orgasm, the joy of feeling that life would start moving again, that time would start to pass again and maybe one day the rape would be a small, faraway dot. Wrapping myself around him, I said, Me, too. He smiled, put his head between my legs and, unlike him, I took my time, I took a long time, I let him stay in the same place for ages. I'd already thought about it and was sure I'd cry a lot, sure I wouldn't last because I'd be crying too much, but suddenly the orgasm came, I came with his tongue on me — and I didn't cry.

Did you know you can also tell your personality from the shape of your mouth, I asked Dulcineia. She looked at me with a certain pity, no doubt thinking I was going crazy, but I wasn't. It's true, I said, I saw it on the internet. You, for example, you have big, thick lips, and people with a mouth like yours were born to care for others. It makes perfect sense, don't you think? Police officers were born to look after other people. Ah, and they also have a strong maternal instinct. Do you have kids? I really want them, but Michel thinks we should wait for the right moment. If we wait for the right moment, we'll never have kids, will we? She agreed, shaking her head. My upper lip is bigger than my lower lip, and people with this shaped mouth are dramatic, emotional, charismatic, and cheerful. Do you think I'm dramatic, emotional, charismatic, and cheerful? I know I'm cheerful. She was silent, so I said, Wait a minute.

I came back holding several laminated sheets, with the illustration and description of a different mouth shape on each. People whose bottom lips are bigger than their upper lips, I said, aren't suited to office work; they can't stay sitting when they know there's a world to explore outside.

On the other hand, I continued, pointing at the page, that's an ugly mouth, isn't it? People with ordinary lips — what nomenclature — are balanced, and know how to resolve problems of any degree of difficulty. Which means, I imagine, that being unbalanced is the exception. People with thin lips are solitary, but they're like that because they want to be, because they like solitude; people whose upper lips have soft curves are compassionate, sensitive, and caring; people with a straight upper lip are the most responsible and self-assured in the world; and those whose upper lip has a strong V shape are creative and excellent at remembering faces and names. I've studied myself in the mirror, but I can't decide if the curve of my upper lip is soft or if I have a strong V. What do you think? It's a bit more of a V than soft, isn't it?

I thought: There are worse things in life. There are people who lose a child in a car accident. There are people who lose their entire family in a landslide. There are people who lose movement in their legs. There are people who lose an arm or a leg. Both arms and both legs. There are people who get burns, and end up completely disfigured. There are people who are raped by ten guys on the same day.

But other people's pain didn't diminish mine.

So I gave up imagining worse tragedies, and did little things that gave me pleasure: feeling the hot sun on my face, sinking my feet into the sand, going for a dip in the ocean at the empty beach on weekdays. A bowl of *açaí* with banana and honey, no syrup, was a delight that I discovered in that period. I would wake up in the morning with the same anxiety as always — the stranger's face very clear in its totality, but diffuse in its details — head down the stairs of my building, walk to the juice bar, and order a large bowl of *açaí* with banana and honey, no syrup. I'd savour it slowly, thinking that not all solitude was bad. I needed to make peace not only with my body and with life, but also with the city.

Two years after our first meeting with city hall, on the eve of the Olympic Games, the golf course designer, one of the most highly regarded specialists in the United States, had arrived in Rio to see how it was coming along. By then, the topography of the eighteen holes was finished, as was the sprinkler system and the dredging of the lakes. The lawn was almost ready. Cadu and I went there with a mixture of enthusiasm and apprehension, because every time we visited the course we ended up arguing with the contractor. His intention to do everything as quickly as possible clashed with our ideas.

When we got there, we were greeted with a peculiar scene that makes me laugh every time I think of it: the designer himself was driving the backhoe, wearing a Walkman, modelling the terrain. He knew better than anyone that the shape of a golf course is hard to plan, because it's landscape, and landscape never bows entirely to one's will. So there he was, operating the backhoe; he was the image of a man who wouldn't accept defeat, the image of desperation, but also of insistence, the will to assure that, in the end, victory would be his.

A few days later, we returned to the golf course to see the stripping of the building's formwork. The process is like this: first you make the form; then you add reinforcement, steel; and then you pour the concrete. After that, you need to wait for it to cure, which takes a few days. A curing blanket stops evaporation, trapping the water in the capillary spaces, hydrating the concrete so it doesn't crack. Then the building is stripped, and the structure appears, raw, for the first time. What you designed on the computer is born before your eyes, much bigger than you.


Right at the beginning of my pregnancy, in the ecstatic joy of expecting two babies, it dawned on me that my existence would be suspended for nine months. I began to crave things I'd never eaten: pasta, rice, potato puree, bread. A hunger greater than my desire for control. That was when I thought: In the months to come, I'll be someone else. One kilo on my body already made a difference, my pants became tight before week twelve, before I could tell people, I'm not fat, I'm pregnant with twins. I loved the idea of becoming a mother, but I hated the transformation of my body. I hated looking in the mirror and not recognising myself.

But I was afraid of harming you, and that fear combined with the feeling that you were saving me. I ate for you, even if my body was expanding forwards and sideways.

My belly grew and, although I always heard that pregnancy suited me, at no point did I feel attractive. Michel was inexplicably turned on, while my libido was sliding downhill: the transformation was an assault to a body that, until then, I'd known how to control.

As the weeks went by, I lost the desire to eat pasta, rice, bread, and potato puree, and opted for a pure, natural diet. The extravagance of my cravings consisted of waking up in the middle of the night wanting to eat cucumber. I only ate organic food, almost no sugar; gluten, no way; milk, only if it was almond or rice milk.

I kept running and working out, as well as doing yoga. Michel would laugh when he came across me squatting in the living room or walking through the apartment on all fours. My belly was growing bigger and bigger, and there I was, still at it — stand, squat — the same exercises that I did for nine hours in the hospital room when I went to give birth.

The nurses would walk in and see me naked, crazy, on all fours on the bed. I'd say, Don't mind me, and they'd pretend it was all very normal. After months of the purest diet and precise exercises, those babies had to come out of my cunt exactly as I'd imagined, preferably without anaesthetic, because the pain of natural childbirth is a sublime pain.

Squeeze hard harder squeeze until he breaks, I repeated in my head as he came and went, I told myself, if I squeeze really hard it'll break, just a little more, hard, break split destroy hard now break rip cut, I looked at his face and thought, it isn't hurting him, harder, I can't do it any harder, yes you can, squeeze squeeze break, his face, his prickly stubble, his mouth, I saw, I see there's a cut on the left side, it's thin, his lips are thin, squeeze hard, it isn't hurting him, it isn't going to break, the cut's bigger than his lip, it extends past his mouth, I'm squeezing as hard as I can, and what if instead of it breaking he likes it?, he can't like it, I don't want him to like it, but he has to like it so he'll go away and leave me to see Michel again so we can get married and my children can exist, it's breaking, I'm sure it's going to break, split in half, but what if half stays inside me?, his beard's patchy his breath is bad I'll never forget it, rotten, reeking, nauseating, hard, just a little more and it'll break.

When I got out of the shower, I found the two of you sitting at my desk, in front of the computer. I ran, yelled at you — me, who never yells, who's such a patient mother, who speaks softly, I gave you a tongue-lashing. Get down immediately, I demanded, wondering, Did they read anything? I know you don't know how to read, but the image, the two of you in front of the computer, in front of these words that you're reading now, if you ever read this letter, disturbed me. You're going to ask, Why tell your children about an act of violence that took place before them?

It's been more than a month since I started writing, and while it's true that I've thought about deleting it all a few times, I haven't. Of course I'd prefer not to tell you. Protect you from any pain. But I could only not tell you if it hadn't happened.

Seeing you upset with me, I remembered the day when Márcia told me, You'll need to talk. She, Márcia, who almost never says anything, said that I needed to talk. Not to the police, but to myself, talk while lying on the divan, with the ceiling before my eyes, really talk, talk about what happened, tell myself what I'd gone through.


The doors and windows of the bungalow were open; the sun had just set. I turned on the lamp on the bedside table and went to get two beers from the bar fridge. Michel, lying in the hammock on the veranda, said it was exactly what he was thinking when I arrived with the beers. Lie down here, he suggested. Coming, I replied. I had an odd feeling, nothing important, just a feeling that, for lack of a name, caused me to wander aimlessly around the room, as if I wanted to distract it, make it pass.

I observed each object, each decoration, the decor that alternated between chic and as natural as possible, the wooden bench and table, the straw chandelier, a ceramic vase with artificial flowers, and suddenly I stopped in front of two masks, a puma and an orangutan. With my eyes closed, I ran my hands over the puma before putting it on my face. I took the hair elastic from my ponytail and used it to secure the mask on my face.

I walked slowly, as if trying to adjust to my new being, and, on the veranda, I called Michel, who was staring at the sea, lost. I heard his timid laughter at the unexpected sight. At that instant, I felt that the mask was perfect on me. He took a sip of beer, said something I don't remember, and we went back to the room, the veranda doors open, the evening breeze arriving.

I felt Michel's erection through his trunks. I rubbed my body against his. He wanted to lift up the mask to kiss me, but I didn't let him. With the mask, I wasn't myself, and it was in this absence from myself that I felt more myself.

Kneeling, I lifted it slightly when I wanted to take Michel in my mouth. Then I heard him say, The door to the veranda, better shut it. I didn't pay the slightest attention. Michel's hard dick in my mouth, the mask, the two of us there on that Caribbean beach, far from everything, the breeze, the idea that someone might see and hear us — I had no desire to close the veranda door.

When I lifted my head, I said, my voice distorted and deep behind the mask, Put on the other one, there's a hair elastic on the table. I waited a while, just listening to his footsteps, the sound of a lighter, the smell of incense slowly rising and, suddenly my body was dragged before falling onto the sofa. When I felt Michel's tongue between my legs, I also felt the mask brushing against my stomach.

We were very aroused, his dick in my cunt, my cunt on his dick, the words sticking to what they represented, relief together with horniness, relief making me horny, horniness making me relieved. We only lifted up our masks from time to time to kiss, but it was a time to time that was repeated many times. We stayed there for a long time, having sex in the cabana, on all fours, lying down, sitting up, spooning, his hands on my body, mine on his, the pleasant smell of his mouth, the moans, the masks, the open veranda doors, the breeze.

A few days after that visit to the police station, I received a photograph of another man. There was no way that, in the flesh, this one would turn out to be my attacker, so I told the assistant it wasn't worth going down to the station. But he insisted and I went, this time alone.

In the same small room, I saw five men in a line-up. I looked at each one carefully, but none of them looked like the identikit sketch. The assistant was calm, as if he knew the culprit wasn't there and that the scene was just staged.

There are things about the process that I don't understand to this day. Was there an objective behind that act? Did they think that by showing me such different portraits I'd end up identifying one that was remotely similar?

Dulcineia didn't even show up. The protocol was as quick and simple as possible, and I left the station feeling jaded. They don't want to find the right man, I thought. Or maybe they thought they'd never find him. Rio de Janeiro is enormous; Brazil is enormous. After so many days, the man was probably hiding in the backlands or a on beach in the north-east, or maybe not even that far, lost in Rio's outer suburbs, or working in Mangaratiba, perhaps; contrary to what I imagined, he might have been married with kids, hard-working, honest, polite, someone who didn't raise the slightest suspicion, and perhaps the suspects taken to the police station were very far removed from who he really was. They stopped sending photographs to my phone. They'd just call me, arrange a time for me to go to the station, and I'd go.

I opened the newspaper and read: a woman had been brutally raped on the way up to Vista Chinesa. Another woman. They said she was a doctor and had been riding a bike up. She did it every morning, normally accompanied by her husband, but on that fateful day she had gone alone, and her bike had been found at the edge of the forest, a little beyond the Wall of Relief, attracting the attention of passers-by, who called the police. The woman was found alive, but seriously injured. She was well now, said the article. The police suspected it was the same man who, not long before that, had raped an architect, and my name was beside the word 'architect,' next to an identikit sketch of the man — a very similar sketch, but not the same one that Dulcineia had taken to my apartment. It was the man himself, my attacker, drawn to perfection. I recognised every feature — the prickly stubble, the nose, the eyes — it was exactly like him. It was him, I saw with such clarity, but suddenly a bloodstain appeared on the newspaper and it spread across the entire page, and the man's face disappeared under the red.

In the room at the police station, three other women and I stared through the glass at four suspected rapists. We'd been attacked in the same place by a short, strong man who wore black or blue gloves. Four men in a line-up. The first woman pointed and said, It's him. The second pointed at another man and said, That one's mine. The voice of the third woman was serious, That one. There was only one man left, and because he was the only one left, I shouted, Guilty! Then the four of us started shouting, banging on the glass, and I felt the cut on my hand, blood trickling, the pain, as if it had just happened, and that was when I leapt out of bed, drenched with sweat. Nightmares gave me no respite.

———

You were both positioned head-down. Even though I knew natural childbirth is more difficult and unlikely with twins, I wanted to try. I wanted to feel you coming out of my vagina, the orgasmic experience described in books and blogs. Additionally, they say that when babies are born naturally they have fewer allergies, they're healthier and more confident. They take to the breast better. And the woman who chooses the natural way, preferably without anaesthesia, is more of a woman, a wonder woman.

On my way to the hospital, I was firm: If at any point I say I don't want anaesthesia, tell the doctor I've gone crazy. The pain was so strong, a knife in my lower back, I hollered like in the movies, thrusting my body forward. In the room, Dr Brito concluded that I was three centimetres dilated. If that was three, imagine what was to come, but Catarina, the doula, had already arrived and convinced me to walk down the corridor before making a final decision. We walked and I screamed, opening my legs like a duck. Breathe, she said, breathe. I breathed, the time between contractions growing shorter. Let's go back, I said, I want anaesthesia, don't be upset with me, I admit my weakness, I hate pain.

I received a low dose so I could keep walking, squatting, doing exercises on the Pilates ball and would have the strength necessary for Martim to come out. Catarina and I held hands. Michel would come in, leave, put on some music, make some work-related phone calls. Time was passing, and Dr Brito told me, The anaesthesia is going to wear off, and I need you to go without meds for a while so we can get this kid lower down. Then a searing pain made me push, and I could feel the goo coming out and running down my legs. They say that when the pain becomes too much, you transcend it.

In the delivery room, in the birthing chair, Martim's hairy head in the palm of my hands, him crowning, me crowning, us crowning life, push, push, push, lots of blood, Michel taking photos, he hates blood, he faints when he sees blood, the camera helps, a buffer between representation and reality, the blood that is and isn't mine, me, an animal, a beast in the jungle, hollering, lots of hollering, Didn't you bring the music? asks Dr Brito, No, I say, no music now, I howl, my howl is the music, my face is the animal, my face is the mask, a mask that roars, I look in front of me, they're wearing masks, too — Michel, Catarina, Dr Brito, the nurse, so many people in the delivery room, so many masks, so many animals — and suddenly the pleasure I'd heard about, a prolonged orgasm, Martim coming out, my orgasm lasts the time he takes to be born, the longest, most intense orgasm, I thought it was hippie talk, impossible to have an orgasm giving birth, but there it is, unexpected pleasure, Martim coming out, I help Dr Brito myself at the final moment and bring the baby to my breast, the blood, the goo, the amniotic liquid, his skin on my skin, the umbilical cord pulsating, Michel, the scissors, the cut, Martim on my breast, sucking my milk, a little mouse born ready, he already knows what to do, ten out of ten, this kid's ten out of ten, what now?, now the placenta's going to come out, and out it comes, a piece of flesh, red, blue, viscous. Some people eat it, some people make capsules out of it, but I just touch it, I need to start over, the baby girl, Antonia, she's about to come out, my vaginal canal open, my cunt open, torn. The second one is easier, just a few minutes and she'll be here, the contractions start again, different, not as strong, not as constant, Push, they chorus, push, but suddenly a strange face, a worried face, quick movements, Call the anaesthetist, the baby's heart is beating too fast, she's suffering and stuck, her head won't turn, it's too risky to try a manoeuvre now, we're going to have to operate, c-section, Oh, no, I thought, my cunt's open and they're going to cut open my belly? Oh, no, I say, but no one hears me, only Michel, who says, The only thing that matters is that she's born healthy. It'll be quick, Dr Brito reassures me, as the anaesthetist injects through the catheter the anaesthesia that makes me groggy this time. I don't feel my legs, nor do I notice when they tie me down like Jesus on the cross, and suddenly everything seems so beautiful, I love everyone, I love the faces in front of me, I feel the scissors lightly scrape my stomach, a slight discomfort, on the mirrored machine above me I can see what the curtain hides, my organs outside of my body, my insides outside of me, and I see Antonia being lifted out, Antonia's out, Antonia wailing, the crying that makes you forget if it was a normal birth or a c-section, the crying that gives meaning to everything that came before and everything yet to come, to everything that has no meaning at all. And after that I don't see anything else, I don't see them put my organs back, I don't see them stitch up my belly, I ask them to untie my arms, and they untie one, the arm that holds Antonia on my chest, while Michel rocks Martim, already bathed and dressed.

In the village we came across a mask shop, and I thought, It can't be a coincidence, before remembering that whenever I discover something, it happens. We went in. There was every kind of mask: faces that were kind of human, kind of monstrous, kind of simian, kind of diabolical, extremely colourful, a gaping, sarcastic smile, a wide-open mouth, teeth on display, as if they were laughing at us, at the faces looking at them, as if they were laughing at all of humanity, at our naivety, at our pettiness, at our self-importance, at our terror of death, at our inability in the face of the inevitable, of the randomness, a mocking smile, a smile of the gods, a superhuman smile, fascinating, seductive, and repulsive at the same time, a smile that you don't want to see but can't stop looking at, laughter that you don't forget. All those masks. All those faces. Those expressions. I thought, If my attacker was exotic, I'd be able to recognise him. But if my attacker was like that among a whole bunch of people like that, I'd have to distinguish him by the absence of red, by the excess of yellow. If he was like that I wouldn't be able to describe him, but I'd be able to recognise him. Would I be able to recognise him? One mask next to another, lots of masks, all looking at me, all laughing at me, that nose doesn't fit any type of nose, that mouth, any type of mouth, the faces on the masks have lots of things that a normal face doesn't have, many details that a normal face doesn't have. A normal face, I thought, he had a normal face, perhaps I could define it precisely like that, a normal face. So many things in my head, always so many things in my head, and suddenly a smile, Michel's smile, a bag in his hand. I bought two, his voice was saying, let's go, his hand, the two of us walking along outside of the shop, a taxi, and the two of us back at the hotel, having sex with our new masks, having sex with that gaping, sarcastic smile, that smile of mockery at humanity.

How many footsteps, I can't say, or how long, I just know that it wasn't nearby, that we walked a lot, at least it seemed like a lot, everything was a lot. I had no idea why he was pushing me into the forest. When the idea of rape occurred to me, it quickly dissipated; of course not, rape, like that, on a Tuesday afternoon, without any warning, without any sign, impossible, but why would he take me so far just for a mobile phone, the only object I had on me? Slowly, my incomprehension gave way to fear. Maybe he was a psychopath whose only objective was to kill me.

The gun pressed to my head, he pulled me along forcefully, dragged me through the forest, the branches scratching me, the trees blocking my view. Every now and then, a word, a phrase, Walk or I'll kill you, and the stench rising through my nostrils, the urge to vomit right there, my legs dragging, staggering but strong, obeying the voice. He was going to kill me, and I didn't want to die.

Then, dread. I wanted everything to be over quickly, still not knowing what that everything was, I wanted things to unfold as swiftly as possible and for me to be back home. One feeling never gave way to another. They piled up.

Suddenly, the forest opened up, I saw a clearing, and I didn't even have time to think. He shoved me to the ground. I fell face-down and turned in reflex, I looked up — so many leafy treetops, so much green, so much brown, so much yellow — and him in front of me, still standing, taking off his pants, his dick hard. His dick hard. I remember thinking, When did he start getting turned on? And what turned him on exactly? Seeing me lost, afraid, nauseated, anxious? Pressing the gun to my head and bringing me to this hidden place where no one, I remember thinking, absolutely *no one* will find us? I didn't scream. I didn't move. I was paralysed. That man without pants in front of me, his dick hard, was too incomprehensible and frightening.

The worst thing was the confirmation. I was going to be raped. He was going to do whatever he wanted to me, and in the end he'd kill me. Why leave me alive in that forest after having taken me so far?

The worst thing was the feeling of anticipation. The knowledge that he was going to do to me whatever he wanted, but had yet to do it.

No. The worst thing was his tongue on my face, a mangy dog licking me.

He tore off my leggings with violence, his rough gloves scratching my skin, and stuck his dick in my cunt. His dick in my cunt. I can't bear to use these words, but I don't know what's more accurate. After all, it was that: it was his dick inside my cunt. But it was anything but that. A dick in a cunt is something else.


A transparent adhesive bandage is stretching my skin from one side of my groin to the other. The pain is excruciating. I ask the nurse to pull it off. She says she can't, but promises to relieve my suffering. She gets some scissors and cuts off a bit of the adhesive. The skin relaxes, but the pain remains. Five minutes later, I ring the bedside bell, I can't take it anymore. The nurse announces that she is going to inject me with paracetamol. I tell her that paracetamol does nothing — they've already put paracetamol into that tube I don't know how many times, and it didn't even touch the pain. She says it's the doctor's orders, and makes a move for my arm. I say, No, if you don't want to give me real medicine, then don't give me anything. She leaves in a huff and reappears a few minutes later with the anaesthetist, who talks to me as if I were a spoiled child. He tells me that he's the doctor and he's the one who knows what I can and can't take. I turn my head to the side and see the two of you sleeping. The anaesthetist's voice irritates me. When he finishes his lecture, I say, You might be the doctor, but it's my body. He looks as me in surprise and I continue, Nine hours of labour, one normal birth and one c-section, a migraine that hurt more than any contraction, I've been cut open, stitched up, and had this adhesive stuck on me. I've already had paracetamol several times. It made no difference. For heaven's sake, give me some real medicine. He gives me a little smile and says, You want some real medicine? I'll give you some real medicine. He winks at Michel, fills the syringe, and injects the liquid into the tube. I feel profound happiness and think, long live morphine, long live opium, long live all drugs.

Then I black out.

A boy a year above us put a plastic gun to Rafael Augusto's head and said, I don't want to, but I'm going to have to do this. Another three burst out laughing, while I looked in astonishment at the boy who pulled the trigger, then I ran away.

Two weeks later, Rafael Augusto came up to me, downcast, and whispered hesitantly, as if apologising, I'm changing schools. We just stood there facing one another, without saying anything. The boy with the problem in his heart was leaving the girl with the headgear. At the age of thirteen, I was already used to feeling alone, but I remember that that day, the school courtyard full of people at recess, I felt a cut, a blade puncturing my chest, the thought piercing me: I don't like being alone.

I don't remember exactly how we ended up at that party, but I remember the party, the place it was held, an enormous warehouse far from the village, an abandoned warehouse where a tall, well-dressed man at the door asked our names, checked a piece of paper, and let us in. It was dimly lit and there was a lot of smoke, not only from cigarettes but also a special effect, like beams of light that crisscross the air. Michel and I looked at each other with a mixture of curiosity and surprise. The decoration was what you would expect of a strange place — a few red sofas scattered around at random, chairs and old tables, some broken, and, on the walls, contemporary paintings alternating with Mayan-inspired craftwork. A few masks. First, I thought they were following me, but then I began to imagine that the masks were part of Tulum's identity.

The further we went and the more we got lost in the different spaces separated by Oriental room dividers, the darker and more enigmatic the place became. Despite the large number of people moving here and there and the loud music, I felt as if everything was happening in slow motion: the woman at the entrance to the dance floor serving us two glasses of water, sprinkling powder in the glasses, a broad smile on her round, brown face, an indigenous face. I drank the water with the dust in it all at once, before looking to see what your father was doing, before he gave me an apprehensive look and followed suit. Inside, there were dozens of people holding glasses and bottles of water. I didn't notice it right away, but there was a small platform at the back, not terribly high, where five or six very young women were dancing. They might have been eighteen or twenty, but they looked younger, as pretty as the woman at the door, some as brown-skinned as her, with very straight, very black hair.

For an instant, I thought, Those girls are very young; for an instant, I wondered, Do they even want to be here? But the powder dissolved in the water didn't take long to take effect, and the next instant all I could think was, those girls are so gorgeous, those girls are so happy, dancing with their sumptuous, beautiful, intact bodies, full of life. I remember looking around me and all I could see was people kissing, men with women, women with women, men with men, multiple kisses, it seemed like everyone was kissing, and I kissed your father.

I grabbed two masks from the wall — nothing we did there shocked anyone — and we rubbed up against one another, his hand under my skirt, the other undoing the buttons on my blouse, my breasts out of my bra, the pleasure of my breasts out of my bra.

I don't remember how much longer we spent at the party, what else we did at the party, where our arousal took us at the party. There's a blank between the two of us dancing, kissing, wearing masks, and my next memory: the two of us in bed and me telling Michel, Fuck me in the arse. I clearly remember the words coming out of my mouth, and I also remember him fingering me as he fucked me in the arse, and his moan and spasms before rolling over and falling asleep.

Behind his prickly stubble were spots, perhaps from pimples. No, he wasn't an adolescent; he was definitely over twenty, maybe thirty, maybe forty. Do I have to pinpoint it? Say Aah, the wooden spatula touching my throat. When I was a child, my doctor's name was Dr Mafra. When I had my first period, I started going to Dr Nadir. There are women who don't like going to male doctors, they don't feel comfortable. During your delivery, drugged, seeing my organs outside of me and hearing the anaesthetist talking about football, I repeated a thought that came and went: My delivery is a scene from a soap opera. Soap writers are right; it really happens. The anaesthetist was a Vasco supporter, and as Vasco was playing that day, he wanted to go to Maracanã Stadium. But with all the violence, in the end it wasn't at Maracanã, it was closed to the public, but I remember him saying he wasn't going because of the violence, how the city had become violent, or maybe I've got it wrong, when you kids were born Maracanã wasn't closed, but the anaesthetist said that, I heard that Vasco was going to play, he wanted to see Vasco play, and suddenly Antonia was out, so beautiful, so perfect. Has she got all her fingers? Martim had baby acne, he was a cute little baby, but his face was covered in spots. Ah, sorry, I didn't mean to change the subject, the stranger, the attacker, it's better to call him that: the attacker, right? He must have had lots of pimples when he was a teenager. I remember well now: I can see him in front of me, they weren't spots, they were pockmarks on his face, under the stubble. Does that help at all?

Ilha Pura, 'Pure Island,' is the name of the most luxurious athletes' village in the history of the Olympic Games. In a space of 800,000 square metres, it was composed of seven condominiums, had thirty-one towers, 3,604 apartments, and state-of-the-art lifts imported from South Korea. For its residents' leisure there was also a wood with several lakes, a skate park, three kilometres of bike paths, and eight multi-sport courts, making it the perfect condominium. In other words, Ilha Pura had everything you needed to enter and never leave. In a 1,000-square-metre sales stand, you could purchase your property for prices that went from 750,000 to three million *reais*. All in the good taste for which Barra da Tijuca — it's actually Jacarepaguá but it sounds fancier to say Barra da Tijuca — is known. After all, the magnate was born in Jacarepaguá, but he's the King of Barra, Mr Olympics, the man who owns six million square metres of land and who in 2014 was building the homes of Rio's elite on Avenida Salvador Allende; imagine that, without any poor neighbourhoods nearby, with gardens of a standard that only kings enjoy, according to the description. Ilha Pura mustn't sully the region's fate, he told the interviewer, and so it needed to house the upper crust, not the poor, while not far from there, in Vila Autódromo, municipal and state authorities were evicting residents; those who didn't want to enter into agreements were wounded with truncheons, rubber bullets, and tear gas as they watched their houses crumble.

The King of Barra wasn't alone in Ilha Pura; half of it belonged to Odebrecht, that pure company, which a short time later would become embroiled in Brazil's biggest corruption scandal. A political crisis, an econômic crisis, and Ilha Pura, financed by the Caixa Econômica Bank, would become the biggest real estate embarrassment in the history of the Olympic Games and of Rio de Janeiro. With only 230 of its 3,604 apartments sold, the syndicate suspended sales even before the Olympics, only to resume in 2018, when it was already the biggest graveyard of new apartments in the city. The flashy sales stand was now modest, with food trucks and no poster girl, and the fuss didn't help. Let's get rid of the name of the owner of the other half, it doesn't look good, and reduce the selling price, the visits to Paris and New York, the purchases at Gucci and Chanel, and the bank repayments; after all, if we're not making money, we can't pay money. The depressed king tripped and fell, cracking his skull and leaving blood all through the room, and lamented the state of his seven little dogs that needed to be fed.

We designed and oversaw the golf clubhouse through to completion, with many arguments and divergences along the way. Back then, we still believed, we were excited by the idea of change, being able to contribute to the city, making the first public clubhouse in Rio de Janeiro. But, of course, it was just a golf clubhouse, and we always knew we weren't doing any more than that. Golf is an elitist sport, and that lawn was always well looked after, mowed, clean. A serene landscape in a neighbourhood that didn't want any surprises.

We wanted to exalt the landscape with a building designed as a large veranda. The golf club is still there. It's beautiful — one day I'll take you to see it. I can say, not without irony, that of all the sports facilities built for the 2016 Olympics, it is the only one still in operation.

Me and a man at the police station, having eliminated the other four straight off. Me and a man with stubble, pockmarks, thin lips, a line on his thin lips, a fair-skinned man, strong, his hair wavy, his nose not very big or very small, his eyes brown, me and an angry man, an angry me and an angry man. Say something, I said. He didn't. Say something, I repeated. He didn't. What's your name? Luiz de Sousa, he replied. What do you do? I'm a street vendor. How old are you? Thirty-three, he said, his anger muzzling his voice, his hatred; he hated me, and I him. Say it again, I ordered. Thirty-three, he repeated, his voice hoarse and deep.

Walk and be quiet or I'll kill you, said the voice, Say you like it, the palm of his hand in my face, the force of the palm of his hand, say it or I'll kill you. My voice: I like it. That's it, my little whore, now repeat it really slowly, I liiiike it. My voice, really slowly: I liiiike it, the first tears along with sobs of fear: I liiiike it. He pulled his dick out of me and hit me, punched me in the face, making his knuckles and my mouth bleed, You lying whore, you're dry. Get wet, a demand — my tears, my sobs, his hand on my tears and then on my cunt, trying to wet it with my tears, but the gloves, the gloves, what kind of gloves, what colour gloves, lick your fingers, that's it, give them a good lick, lick lots, I want to see your tongue, his hand on my arm demanding that I lick my own fingers, my hand on my cunt, my fingers in his mouth, touching his tongue, my fingers on my cunt, my voice in my head, praying, Get wet get wet so this hell can come to an end, his dick in my cunt again, his dick the biggest thing you can stick in a woman's cunt, pain pain pain, him licking my face, ordering me to say: I like it. My obedience: I like it. My thought: He's going to come. My prayer: He's going to come. The interruption, his dick out of me again, the gun in my mouth, this is the worst moment, knowing I'm going to die. My mum, my dad, my brother, Michel, it'll be terrible for those left behind, I don't know when they'll find my body, in what state they'll find my body, but for me it's all going to end, the gun in my mouth, my mouth open, the gun in it, the cold gun, one second for my brain to explode, mixing with the leaves, the snakes, the monkeys, and the jackfruits, Pull the trigger, I thought, Shoot, I prayed, a full stop, I don't want to live after today, I don't want to see anyone, tell anyone, I don't want to resurrect myself, kill me, don't kill me, my parents won't be able to take it, I'd rather die than have to live after this, I prefer to live, don't kill me, yes, kill me, pull the trigger now, explode my mouth, my head, explode this story, no, wait, not yet, I need to get out of here alive, how many things can you think in a few seconds?

Repeat thirty-three. Thirty-three, the hoarse, deep voice of the man at the police station. Now tell me to say I like it. Say you like it. The loathing on the man's face — can you distinguish between types of loathing? Now lick my face, I ordered. The silence, the inertia. Lick my face, I repeated, the silence, the inertia, my growing anger, my voice harsh and dry, lick. The lick, his tongue on my face, his smell, the smell of his breath, the police officer separating us, the officer dragging the man away, me in

Dulcineia's arms, me sobbing in Dulcineia's arms, It isn't him, it isn't, please, don't insist, I want to go home.

Would telling all the details be telling you how long he spent on top of me, how many times he stuck his dick in my cunt and pulled it out again, the gun in my mouth, how many forwards and backwards movements he made until the moment he grabbed me forcefully and ordered me to sit on him?

Him lying down and me on top, him lying down, me on top, I took off running, desperate, I must have taken a few steps, how many I don't know, I don't remember — a few — he grabbed me, pressed me against a tree, and shoved the gun in my mouth as far as my throat, the 38, 82, 85, 444 touching my throat, the gag reflex. Are you crazy? Do you wanna die? He hit me over the head with the gun, I stumbled, fell to the ground, almost passing out. He backed off and came back with the belt, he whipped me with the belt, on the legs, on the arms, on the stomach, he tied my hands behind my back, tore my T-shirt as I was getting up, took off my bra, and started licking my breasts.

I can still feel the texture of his tongue, rougher than the gloves.

Lying on the moist earth, he put me back on top of him. The pain. The pain. The pain.

I'll never forget the pain. My torn skin. My open flesh. So long, it all took so long. Me on top of him, covered in blood, blacking out, hands tied back, repeating the mantra: I like it. His face, it would be impossible to forget his face, there might be a thousand theories about trauma, but Dulcineia's thing of opening and closing your eyes, telling me over and over that I might have forgotten, that I might not remember properly, that people change — I'd never forget that face looking at me, tongue out like a hungry dog, ordering me to repeat, I like it, and every time I closed my eyes he'd order me, open them, I want you looking at me. Tell me I'm hot, say it. You're. Say it. Hot. The whole thing. You're hot. Now ask me to fuck you. Silence. Ask me, the gun to my stomach, the gun to my belly. Fuck me. Very good, he said, that's what I like.

He demanded that I lick his face, my tongue on his prickly stubble, having a hard time keeping my balance with my hands tied behind my back, my grandma's necklace, the necklace with the pendant of the goddess Ixchel, the necklace she'd brought from Mexico bumping against his chin, his neck, and suddenly it was all very fast, I felt him yank off my necklace and toss it away, then I felt more helpless than ever, more unprotected, and I let my body collapse on his.

Come, said my shaky voice, because it was all that I wanted, for him to climax and for that hell to end.

He pushed me to the ground forcefully, untied my hands, and hit me again with the belt. Hell has no end. I tried to understand his logic, predict what he would or wouldn't do, but there was an abyss between my thoughts and his acts. I shouldn't have said anything, I thought, and I didn't want to think anything else, my mind switched off, in darkness until it ended, or until the darkness of death didn't allow me to see, feel, or think anymore.

But the pain, the story that at some point you transcend the pain, that you pass into another sphere, for me the pain was an absolute presence, the pain was my body, the present, the voice telling me, This is happening now, the impossibility of escaping to another time, of not being there.

And, amid slaps, punches, belt, the tear that I imagined ran all the way to my uterus, the man made me get on all fours thinking I'd be able to support my weight, that my body wouldn't collapse on the ground. I wanted to do everything he told me to, for him to feel pleasure, and for the conclusion, still obscure, to show its teeth, but I fell and he didn't care, he kept at it, hard and fast. Did Dulcineia really think I could forget that pain? That smell? That voice? That face? No one was more interested in forgetting than me. To forget was all that I wanted, all that I couldn't do, can't do.

When he came, I felt the pain in the roots of my hair, which he was tugging on. I was disgusted by that limp, heavy body on mine, and my fear was growing at a blood-curdling speed: the end had come. What was next?


Death is tiring, was what I told myself as I walked into that house in the middle of the Mexican forest. Michel and I were the only ones speaking Portuguese, but they seemed to understand us without any effort, just as we understood them. The man who was going to conduct the ceremony introduced himself, and after a long speech about peyote — the psychoactive cactus that certain indigenous tribes had used for thousands of years in sacred rituals to ask for a good harvest, to celebrate births and birthdays, to bring health, and also at funerals, because for them life is cyclical, it ends in order to begin again — he said that in the Yucatec language Tulum means 'wall,' 'trench,' 'barricade,' 'fortification,' but before it was given this name it was called Zama, the city of sunrise, of dawn, of rebirth. In fact, he said, a lot was said about the Mayan calendar's predicted end of the world, that in 2012 the world was going to end, but the Mayans' idea of the end of the world was different from ours; to them, the end always implies a new beginning. So while it is true that the world didn't end, it is also true that the world is ending and that in this end time we need to make contact with our inner selves. Chewing peyote is a way to dive into a reality as unknown as it is intimate, a trip inside each of us.

In the oldest indigenous tradition, the ritual began with the harvesting of the cactus, when great distances were walked. Along the way, the shaman would tell stories of the ancestors and ask for protection for the rest of the journey. The cactus was always considered sacred for its ability to stop the Mayans from feeling hunger, thirst, or fear. Once back with the tribe, the ceremony would carry on into the night, with lots of singing and dancing and people ingesting peyote. The songs were a form of prayer, of asking for protection; the cactus, the path to visions, to people connecting with what is most ancestral, the earth itself, the jungle, the forest. Many of you here today, he continued, have already heard this story, but we have guests who are going to experience this deeper reality for the first time, and I like to explain to the newcomers the origins of our ritual, which, although it isn't religious — we don't practise any religion here — is somewhat religious in the sense of connection, reconnection, of communion with the earth. When he said that, I stopped paying attention and felt a little afraid, wondering if I should really be there. I remember holding Michel's hand for the last time before we separated: men on one side, women on the other. He explained that our energies were different and worked better if there was a little distance between them, and that was how I suddenly found myself surrounded by women — not many, about six. That was also when I began to feel reassured, especially when one of them explained that she wasn't going to eat the cactus so she could take care of us.

I was the first to take one of the peyote buttons from the glass bowl after analysing its strange appearance, which varied a lot in size and consistency — some round, others long, all brown in colour. I chose the one that looked the smallest, and waited for everyone to take theirs, when I heard a voice beside me say, *Masque,*

*masque, esto se masca* — Chew, chew, you chew it. My hand perspired when I raised the button to my mouth. I remained motionless for a few seconds before following the instructions of the woman near me. I tasted a terrible bitterness together with the feeling that my tongue and lips were going to sleep, until my whole mouth was numb, which made me chew faster and faster, as if by moving it the feeling would go away. After a while, my mouth was so numb that I could no longer taste the bitterness of the cactus. Then I felt like I was at the top of a roller-coaster at the exact moment when the car finishes its ascent, stops for a few seconds, and you ask yourself: What am I doing here?

The button was quite stringy, and I wasn't sure if I should spit it out or swallow it. A violent thirst invaded me and I tried to ask for water, but my voice wouldn't come out. Then the woman who was taking care of us — another name I've forgotten, because I'm good at remembering faces but terrible with names — appeared with a bowl of water, saying that we could refresh ourselves, but we couldn't drink. I rinsed my mouth and spat out the water. I was still in this world, but my heart was accelerating.

The transition took place gradually. When I realised I was being taken, I began to shake my head from side to side, trying to say that I didn't want to go, I didn't want to lose control of my awareness, but it's like a roller-coaster, impossible to get off when you're at the top. I remember seeing our guardian's smile, feeling her light hand stroking me before I surrendered to the effects of the peyote.

A few men were playing musical instruments as they sang with some women. The first thing I saw were their hands growing until they were deformed, bigger than the guitar, than the drum; I saw their faces become deformed, disproportionate noses, hair standing on end. I felt relieved that they were on the other side of the room. I managed to change my gaze to the women around me, and they were beautiful, sweet, with garlands of flowers on their heads. They comforted me, giving me a feeling of peace that slowly turned into a sublime happiness, so sublime that when I looked back at the men I found their monstrosity terribly funny. I no longer felt distressed, and I began to laugh. I laughed until I was out of breath.

Images would appear in front of me, and I would laugh. Image after image, deliriums that made me understand 'Lucy in the Sky with Diamonds,' mushrooms, forest, colourful pictures, birds, lots of movement, and always the feeling of peace, of harmony, a happiness I'd never felt before. I've never been so happy, I thought. The women beside me began to appear in my head, in front of me. We made a circle, and I was placed in the centre, pregnant, my belly enormous, the joy of having a baby in my womb, and suddenly a streak of blood, I opened my legs, and what came out of me was my uterus, the uterus that the goddess Ixchel picked up off the ground, upside down, making the blood gush out even more. As she ran off with my uterus, the serpent on her head hissed and stared at me with loathing; and just like that, my supreme happiness turned into profound sadness. I've never been so sad, I thought.

The women slowly left, following Ixchel, and when I found myself alone I also saw myself with the man's face. I couldn't wake up, but I was very awake. The image became clearer and clearer: my body with the face of the man, the stranger, the rapist. I saw his face with a clarity that I hadn't before, not even the day it happened. I started clawing at my face, which was the man's face, to tear off his skin, his nose, his mouth, to disfigure the face that was taking over my body, but the skin repaired itself each time, the face reassembled itself every time I tore it up. Contrary to what happened after my dreams, the man's face didn't disappear: it came back, insisted, recomposed itself.

Then I felt a hand pulling me outside, taking me for a walk in the forest, barefoot, that hot night. I don't think we walked very far, but every tiny stretch was a long journey. Things grew, I could see the details of where I was — the paws of tiny insects, the sap of plants, the slightest movement, nothing escaped me. When I thought the effect of the peyote was going to wear off, I felt the earth rising beneath my feet, the tree roots stretching, bending, until they reached my legs, pulling me down, slowly burying me, as if my body was going to disintegrate in the forest, and suddenly I felt breathless, the roots wrapping around my neck, and I couldn't breathe. I raised my hands to my grandma's necklace — maybe that was what was strangling me — and tried unsuccessfully to take it off. I was only able to breathe again when I felt the woman's hand pulling me, when I heard her voice saying, Come, let's walk, a sweet, tender voice that calmed me, that took me from distress to a feeling of peace.

I spent the night between the deliriums that came and went, between happiness and sadness. The return to my normal state was tranquil, clear, and soft. The men stopped looking like monsters, and the women no longer brought me any special comfort. Shortly before the sun came up, we drove to a *cenote*, a subterranean pool. Despite the beauty of the place, without the effect of the cactus, I no longer felt so connected to nature. I picked my way awkwardly over the rocks, tripping, making small pauses, thinking before taking a step forward.

There was no one there but us. The cave was an enormous gaping mouth with crystal-clear blue water inside it. We swam, and talked about the experience. Michel had vomited all night and hadn't had a single vision. He also hadn't liked the music or the bitter flavour of the peyote. When he told me how worried he'd been when he saw me standing there in the forest, screaming that I couldn't breathe, I raised my hand to the necklace, and my distress came back. I knew, then, that I needed to return to the place we'd just come from, to the place in the forest where that feeling had paralysed me.

A busload of tourists was arriving as we left the

*cenote*. We followed the car in front of us and, back at the house where we'd spent the night, I asked my guardian to point me in the direction of the place where I'd felt suffocated. I wanted to be alone to dig a hole in the earth, then I took off the necklace and slowly laid it in the hole before covering it and scattering leaves over it, until it was unrecognisable.

Now, as I tell you this story, I realise that mourning is like that: you bury things in the forest, you bury them in analysis, you bury them in work, you bury them in the life that follows, but there's always a part of them that returns.

On the phone, Dulcineia asked me to go to the Gávea police station to identify a suspect. I didn't have a good feeling about it. That morning, I'd scratched my car on a post on the street where my office is, Márcia had cancelled our session, and I'd burned my tongue on my coffee — little things that together gave me the disturbing feeling that it was going to be a bad day.

But I couldn't put it off. If I arranged to go the next morning, the man would have to spend the night at the station. I asked Diana to go with me. She came to my office, and we went together.

How much time had passed since the start of the investigation? How many times had I gone to the police station? Each time, the same upheaval, reliving the horror, imagining the face that I just wanted to forget, hearing the voice that I just wanted to forget, signing papers, seeing Dulcineia and her assistant. Would the guy ever be caught? Or was I just prolonging the suffering?

When the car stopped at traffic lights, Diana took my hand and said, I think it'll be him this time. I smiled. A smile full of pain.

Once I'd filled out the papers, Diana stayed at the door while I was taken in by a police officer I didn't know. I asked if Dulcineia was there, and he told me she couldn't make it, as she had a last-minute commitment.

It really was a bad day. The pieces didn't fit together.

He explained the procedure to me as if I didn't already know it off by heart, and told me that the guy would walk into the room alone. There would be no one else to confuse me. It was important that I observed the details well and remembered that people change, that he could have done things to change his body to throw off the police. Therefore, no similarity should be dismissed.

He came into the room with me, and I immediately knew something was wrong. I'd been to Gávea before, and this wasn't the same room.

They say that dyslexics, as a result of their difficulties with language processing, often develop above-average abilities with images and numbers. I'd already told Dulcineia this, that I don't forget images. In a normal situation, she said. In a normal situation, you might not forget, but in a situation where there is trauma, the person blocks them. There are lots of studies on it. After trauma, the memory creates random blocks. You might be refusing to remember and not even realise it.

On the one hand, I was sure that if I were to come face to face with the stranger, I'd be able to identify him. On the other, Dulcineia's certainty filled me with doubt: what if I got it wrong? What if I had blocked his face? What if I were to blame an innocent man? Or let the real culprit slip past?

It definitely wasn't the same room. It was very bright, and the one I was usually in was dark. I glanced sideways, and out of the corner of my eye caught sight of the mirrored glass. He'd taken me to the wrong room, as if I were the suspect. Was the man now watching me through the glass? Nervous and shaking, I screamed, You've switched us!

The officer narrowed his eyes at me until I pointed up and he saw it. Serenely, he replied, You're right, and led me out of the room without apologising.

Then the strangest thing happened. I knew, as everyone does, that Rio's police force has its shortcomings. But then it happens to you. And you learn personally just how shoddy it can be. That's the word for it: shoddy.

The suspect and I changed places at the same time. I left the room with the one-way mirror, and he left the observation room. And we passed each other right in the middle of the narrow hallway, almost bumping into one another. I looked at him, and he looked at me. Now he knew the face of the person who had caused him to be at the police station with a possible accusation of rape.

In the dark room, I observed the man standing in the well-lit room. He was staring at the wall in front of him, but it was as if he was staring at me. He hated me. He wanted to make it clear that he hated me. I could see it in his eyes. He wasn't at all like the rapist, and I had known it the minute we passed one another in the hallway, his eyes seeking mine.

When I was leaving the police station with Diana, I saw the man's wife and daughter, a girl who couldn't have been more than eight years old. They were crying. Crying because the girl's father had been taken to the police station after a neighbour had reported him. He had recent burns on both hands, and was wearing gloves.

Outside, I burst into tears, too. I felt nauseated, again.

At home, when I started to talk, Diana already imagined what I was going to say. Of course I wanted to see the man who had raped me behind bars. I was angry, and wasn't ashamed to feel angry. But I couldn't bear the idea that the harm that had befallen me might authorise me to bring harm on others. That woman and that girl crying — I'd reached my limit.

I just want to be free to finish my journey, I told Diana. To mourn the part of me that's lost. She heard me, and agreed it was the best thing to do. Those trips to the police station, the phone calls, and the anxiety that was generated each time I went to recognise someone weren't allowing me to move on. Somewhere inside, it felt like abandoning the investigation would be admitting defeat and making me a number: one more raped woman, one less attacker locked up. I hated dropping something in the middle; I always had. Ever since I was little, I'd trained myself to get to the end of everything I'd begun, and successfully. But that day I realised that weakness was the strength that I needed.

I asked Diana not to tell anyone. I wanted to make the decision on my own. That was important, too. When I felt like my life was beginning to belong to me again, then I would tell my parents and Michel. They would support me. After all, they were tired, too. They missed me, too.

RIO DE JANEIRO STATE GOVERNMENT

DEPARTMENT OF PUBLIC SAFETY — DPS

CIVIL POLICE CHIEF

19th Police District

Rua Gal. Espírito Santo Cardoso, 208, Tijuca,

Rio de Janeiro, 20530-500, telephone: 2332-1644

STATEMENT

Internal control.: 068387495-1023/2014

Procedure: 019-06363/2014

Date: 24/08/2014 at 16:21

Name: JÚLIA GUEDES MANSUR (victim)

Nationality: Brazilian

Place of birth: RIO DE JANEIRO

D.O.B.: 07/04/1981

Skin colour: White

Marital status: Single

ID: 1082629-7 IFP, issued on 12/04/2007

Parents: MILTON MANSUR and LÚCIA MONTEIRO GUEDES

Residential address:

Rua Marquês de Sabará, 88 — apt. 101,

Jardim Botânico — Rio de Janeiro, RJ — Brazil

Legally binding:

Impeachment (NONE):

Affirmation:

When questioned, THE DECLARANT SAID:

*She has been very shaken by the crime and, as a result, is no longer interested in proceeding with the investigation, since remembering the event causes her to revisit considerable trauma, triggering constant revictimisation.*

*She also stresses that she wishes to resume her life and would not like to participate in further eyewitness identification procedures, by photograph or in person; she says that due to the stress she was under at the time of the crime she cannot be entirely sure if a given suspect is the true author of the crime. That is all.*

With nothing further to add, the declarant has requested that the Police Authority conclude the present statement, which, having read and approved it, she has signed as the Victim.

I, JUSSIARA RAMOS PINTO, clerk nominated for this act, registration no. 506 971-4, have written and signed.

He dressed slowly. I lay motionless, in the same position, waiting for the bullet. I was going to die face-down, eyes closed. I heard the sound of his pants, belt, shoes, and as soon as there was silence, I heard his voice again, the voice I can't forget, ordering me to stay still for the next fifteen minutes, and suddenly he took off, running. He knows the forest, I thought, he knows the terrain, he knows where he's going, there's a deftness in his footsteps. This isn't the first time he's done this, I thought, other women had felt that terrible solitude.

At that moment in which I almost died, I died. He left, and I was dead. I remember turning over, staring at the sky and feeling that I'd died, seeing the stars, hearing the sound, as if something were separating from my body. I was departing.

I didn't know how to count the time. I didn't know what fifteen minutes were. Just like when I say, We're going in fifteen minutes, and you don't understand. I say, Fifteen minutes, and one minute later you ask, Is it time, Mummy?

As I was getting dressed, an unexpected thought came to me: the waterfall. I wanted to put myself under the cold water and become part of the forest. I didn't want to leave the forest and face the people who would be looking for me. I couldn't find my trainers, my bra, or my mobile. I looked and looked, but nothing. He must have taken them, I thought, as I looked up and saw that the light was dissipating, night, falling. I started remembering the people who die, lost in the forest, hungry, thirsty, cold, attacked by snakes or other animals. I'd survived, and didn't want to die because I couldn't find my way out of there. I didn't know where I was — we'd walked a long way, but which way? I ran, ran along paths that looked more trodden, that looked like trails, I ran clapping my hands, shouting so that someone would hear me as well as the animals. I'd learned that early; my mother had taught me that in the forest, if you don't want animals near you, you have to make noise, because animals don't like people.

It was almost night when my feet returned to the asphalt, now bare, gashed by branches. Finally, I'd found the road. I don't know how long I spent lost in the forest, disoriented, wandering this way and that, watching the sky grow dark at a frightening speed, until I found it, I found the asphalt, and the asphalt had never seemed so soft, so welcoming, so close. I was alive, that's what I was thinking: I'm alive. It was the only thing that mattered. I wanted to get to a safe place and tell people: I'm alive.

A new life, I thought, a new beginning, but what I really wanted was to go back, forget, flee, pretend that nothing had happened. I'd just gone for a run and was on my way back now, it was still light out, a multitude of birds singing happily in the forest, I was sweaty, the pleasure of the endorphins was spreading through my body, Severino would be back from lunch by now and would open the door to the building the minute he saw me, I would greet him as I reached for the key hidden in the pot plant, head up the stairs at a clip, shower, put on some elegant clothes, light makeup, discreet perfume, get my bag, close the front door, get in the car, and arrive on time for the meeting with City Hall, where people would look at me, find me attractive, and listen to all the interesting ideas I'd just had as I was heading home from Vista Chinesa, about the construction of the Olympic golf course clubhouse, certain that I was making Rio de Janeiro a better city.

She is waiting for me at the entrance to the forest, in a long, well-worn skirt, a cloth over her shoulders, her hair black, her skin aged. She doesn't look me in the eye, nor does she answer me when I greet her. With a gesture, she asks me to sit. After saying a few things in a language that is unfamiliar to me, she waves a sprig of herbs over my head and shoulders, then she begins to shake me, and the words she utters become a kind of chant that I sense are a prayer.

In Spanish, she says that I'm carrying a lot of sadness, but that the sadness is beginning to dissipate. You have a strong heart and mind, she says. You don't die easily. You have the spirit of an ancestor in your body. My grandma?

I ask. She doesn't answer. Maybe she doesn't want to name the spirit, I think, but then she says, You did the right thing returning to the earth what belonged to the earth. That's why you've come here. If something bad happens to you, and I know it already has, the spirit will protect you, as the light that relieves the terror. I swallow my tears. I don't know if she notices, because she continues, When life was hard, it saved you. Pay homage to those who came before you, she says without looking at me; she never looks at me. Talk to them. Here, we bury our dead beneath our dwellings. It was they who didn't let you die. Then she breathes slowly, closes her eyes as if trying to decipher a thought, and continues. Where do you live? In Brazil, I reply. Maybe you should leave, she concludes. I shake my head, incredulous. After a moment, she says with confidence that there are two children in my womb. She says this as she rests a hand on my belly and analyses it as if it were a map: *Son dos niños iguales*, they're two identical children.

Why me? I wondered innumerable times. To make me pay attention to my surroundings? To make me be careful and not go to deserted places alone? To make me suffer a physical pain that women have suffered for centuries? To put a stop to my obsession with thinness?

There is no answer that mitigates the violence. There is no answer that convinces me.

There are moments when I can't stop thinking that if I hadn't gone for a run that afternoon, none of it would have happened.

But then I also tell myself that if I'd gone earlier, something worse might have happened. Sometimes I go as far as to think, absurdly, that if I hadn't been raped, the two of you wouldn't exist. The so-called butterfly effect. We'll never know what life might have been if it wasn't what it is.

Was there an element of chance in this event that destroyed and continues to destroy me? Beyond a doubt. But there is something that goes beyond chance: that man's hatred, that man's violence, the permission he gave himself to violate my body. That wasn't chance. That was my random encounter with evil.

Many people pass through here without ever encountering it. When I look at you, I think about it, I'm afraid, and I pray that neither of you ever encounter the frightening face of evil, the face you can never remember but can't forget. I pray that it never repeats itself with Antonia, that it never happens to Martim, that you both grow up believing that evil is a friend who lies, a tooth that hurts, a love that ends.

To be honest, I don't know if I'll ever have the courage to give you this letter, to tell you that your mother isn't just your mother, that your mother is also a woman who has been face to face with the devil.

———

In your bedroom, as well as the photograph in which Michel and I are wearing masks in the forest, there is one of us in Tulum, with the transparent blue sea as our backdrop. I like to think I conceived you on that day. It wasn't long before my body began to show the signs, with everything in double — the nausea, the fatigue, the swelling, until the doctor confirmed at the first ultrasound that there were two. Michel almost passed out. I heard the echo of the voice: *dos niños iguales*, two identical children. But it was a boy and a girl, the boy and the girl that everyone wants and I now cherish.

You know this story. I've already told you. And I'm going to tell it again and again throughout the years. The story of the joyful trip on which you were conceived, of that far-away paradisiacal place that wed me to your father forever.

I had just received an email from Michel with our tickets to Mexico when a storm broke over Rio de Janeiro. I was in my apartment in Horto, and decided to sleep there alone. Rainy nights give me a comforting feeling of peace.

Five years later, the scene repeats itself. But now I live in another apartment on the edge of Jardim Botânico, I'm married, and I'm your mother. Clouds are gathering in the sky at a frightening speed and I know, because the newspapers announced it this morning, that there's going to be a storm. Michel raced out to fetch you kids from school. The last few times it happened, the city entered a state of emergency.

Meanwhile, at the window, I listen to the wind roar over the trees as I wait for the rain to arrive — that sweet, wet smell that comes before a storm.

There were thunderstorms in Rio de Janeiro when I was a child, too. The city would quickly flood, and we'd have to stay wherever we were until the water level went down. I remember being stuck at the São Luiz Cinema, having to pee in a plastic bottle in the car, cockroaches climbing up a woman's legs on Rua das Laranjeiras, dirty water coming through the car window, my father growing nervous as our taxi drowned in a hole, the candles lit at home, and the sound of thunderclaps outside.

But back then, when storms came, after a few hours you could get about again. There was always a moment when the city went back to being what it was like before.

Rio will never go back to what it was like before; my mother repeats this every time she talks about the Copacabana of old, before there was a beach promenade, the short stretch of sand, the sea right there, the low buildings, the trams, the calm traffic, practically a village.

Your father has just called. It has already started raining in the high part of Jardim Botânico. He doesn't know if he should race home, or wait at the school for the weather to ease.

Through the window, I see the clouds approaching. The instant that precedes events, what has already been and what has yet to be. The wait. The forgetting.

At the window, as the heat thickens the air, I forget. I forget myself.

The rain falls, fast. I hear the thunderclaps. The plump raindrops echo down the pavement. It's raining hard. Soon, Michel will call me to say that you're stuck at the top of Rua Lopes Quintas, the street's a waterfall, everything is being washed away — cars, bicycles, trees, people adrift in improvised boats. He's had to abandon the car with you, you've been rescued and taken to the fire station, drenched, you're crying and asking for me and saying you want to come home; there are other children there, other adults, more and more. We stay in contact until his phone battery runs down, but not before he tells me that everything is under control, there are blankets, bread, and water, you're going to spend the whole night at the fire station, while the rest of the city collapses, while your mother writes, a cup of tea on one side and a glass of whisky on the other, a blanket over my knees and the sound of the rain outside.

Three months have passed since the day I began to write this letter, and I don't know if it will ever be delivered.

I've never resigned myself to the idea that a single moment can change a person's life forever and that, by changing that person's life, it also changes their children's lives. The fact would be less terrible if I could just not carry it any further. If the horror could remain in that day, that time, that place.

I don't want to be the person to tell you that, no matter how beautiful, everything has a monster lurking within it.

Two trees have fallen here in the street. Through the window, I see at least three cars that have been destroyed. It's the deluge, and the electricity goes out right this instant. The battery icon on the computer says I only have 12 per cent left and I fret, having decided to finish this today. I've been a little absent, and I think you're beginning to sense it. I remember when I was little and felt that my mother was disappearing, even though she was right there, in the house she still lives in.

A news alert pops up beside the words I am writing, announcing that on Estrada Dona Castorina, better known as the road to Vista Chinesa, which connects Horto to Vista Chinesa, the article explains, there has been a landslide. The road has collapsed, the asphalt has caved in, and the entrance to Tijuca National Park, one of Rio de Janeiro's most beautiful vistas, a postcard of the city, has been sealed off. No one can enter; no one can leave. I watch the video: an enormous hole has opened up in the asphalt in front of the Macacos Weir, close to the Horto waterfalls. In the background, trees are being swept away by the current, the river water mixing with the rainwater, mud sliding down through the forest, the forest itself sliding down through the forest, sweeping away branches, *ipê*, and jackfruit trees, coral snakes, boa constrictors, spiders, lizards, iguanas, capuchin monkeys, agoutis, opossums, sweeping away my bra, my mobile, the strand of hair that was never found, sweeping away the clearing, disfiguring the landscape. The asphalt of the section that collapsed had been sitting on an old arch bridge made of solid stone and brick, built to cross the Rio Pai Ricardo in the mid-nineteenth century, an era in which the only things that travelled that way were people, horses, and carriages. They believe the landslide was caused by vehicle traffic, the asphalt that was laid over it, tree roots and plants growing in cracks in the construction, letting water in, which in turn swamped the soil, sweeping everything away, plants, animals, objects left there, the clearing, sweeping away the man, the man's face, the memory of the man's face, and suddenly I think that the violence suffered on that soil, the violence suffered by that soil, will spill from it; along with the water, mud, and trees, the pain, bones, and flesh torn there will also slide away, sweeping away the stories, the memory, while fire-truck sirens invade my ears and I tell myself that salvation will come from the earth or not, the forest invading and devouring the city, the forest eating the asphalt. Rio's salvation is, always has been and always will be, its own death.

*June 2019*

# Author's note

In 2014, a friend I call a sister was raped while running to Vista Chinesa. A long police investigation to find the perpetrator ensued. I wasn't in Brazil at the time, and was only able to stay abreast of this painful process by telephone, which was the closest form of contact available to me.

At an exhibition a few months later, in early 2015, I saw the series *The Innocents* by American photographer Taryn Simon, which documents a number of cases of wrongful conviction in the United States, raising the question of photography's function as credible evidence. The portraits of people who had been wrongfully convicted based on identification by victims reminded me of my friend's rape and the search for the perpetrator. Her difficulty in establishing whether a suspect was or wasn't the culprit, her reticence to incriminate an innocent man, the police's determination to arrest someone — I couldn't stop thinking about it. That was when I began taking notes to write a novel.

I set the notes aside until the beginning of 2018, when I discovered I was pregnant with a girl, and I thought the time had come to turn them into a book. In order to do so I needed to interview my friend, but I wasn't sure if she would be willing to re-open such deep wounds. The feminist movement had since given her opportunities to talk about the subject, but she had preferred to keep her story among a close circle of people.

As soon as we began a series of interviews, I was surprised by the urgency with which she narrated the experience. The wounds weren't just deep — they were at the surface, on her skin, still very much open and raw. She became so involved in the process that it would have been impossible to interrupt it in the middle. For a time, we established the following routine: she would tell me the story and I would take notes; then I would write, and she would read what I'd written; she would comment on it, and I would revise it. When I felt I had what I needed, I would move on.

I made it clear that I was going to write a novel, and she never interfered with my choice. She never asked me to tell it this way or that way. At a certain point in the process, she asked me only to say that it was a novel based on true events.

When the book was ready, she came to the conclusion that it wasn't enough to merely set forth the facts. She felt it was important to reveal to whom those facts belonged. Would you like me to name you? I asked. Yes, she replied. For months, I played the Devil's advocate, trying to ascertain that it was what she really wanted, until the day she told me: *I'm not ashamed of what happened. I want you to write that this really happened — and that it happened to me, Joana Jabace.*

# Acknowledgements

To Joana Jabace, for the courage with which she told me her story and for the attention she gave to my insistence on the details.

To Leandro Sarmatz, for the enthusiasm and dedication with which he received this book.

To Dina Salem Levy, Paloma Vidal, Mirna Queiroz, Susana Moreira Marques, Eric Nepomuceno, Elisabete Pinto Guedes, Maria Mendes, Bárbara Manfroni Souza, Camila Pitanga, Simone Elias, Sandra Rocha, Lucia Murat, Pedro Rivera, Anabela Mota Ribeiro, Patrícia Melo, Olivia Byington, Antonia Pellegrino, Fabiana Díaz, Claudia Lage, Julián Fuks, Pilar del Río, Adriana Varejão, João Constâncio, Jordi Roca, and Nicole Witt, who, each in their own way, helped make these pages exist.

To Virginia Woolf, W.G. Sebald, Sophia de Mello Breyner Andresen, Carlos Castañeda, and Franz Kafka, for the borrowed words.

To Pedro, with whom I share the beautiful and difficult moments of every book.

To Francisco and José, who have the luck of being Joana's children.

To Nino, the nephew I wish was closer to me.

Once again, to Dina and Joana, for the day we decided to call ourselves sisters.